Without Love

by

Theresa Stillwagon

Without Love

Cover Art by *RJ Morris*

The Wild Rose Press, Inc.
PO Box 708
Adams Basin, NY 14410-0708
Visit us at www.thewildrosepress.com

Publishing History
First Champagne Rose Edition, 2018
Print ISBN 978-1-5092-1932-2
Digital ISBN 978-1-5092-1933-9

Published in the United States of America

"My uncle is right, Mr. Benjamin."

"Luke," he said, surprising her with his sign of friendship. Why he wasn't letting her go was beyond him. Nothing good could come from getting to know this woman better. "My first name is Luke."

Her eyes widened before she smiled gently. "My name is Emma."

"Emma," he said, loving the sound of the name. "What actually was your uncle right about?"

"That it's time you stopped getting that…brother of yours out of bad situations," she whispered, gaze tracing heated interest over his face. "Mark doesn't look anything like you."

He swallowed and stayed quiet as she spread that penetrating look down his body and then up again. Like with a touch of real fingers, he reacted in a real way. Thankfully the table blocked his lower body from her view. He sighed when she finally focused onto his heated face again. A sweet, slight flush warmed her cheeks for a brief moment.

Damn, why did this woman have to make him start feeling? Why did the woman carrying his brother's child make him aware of how long it'd been since he felt a female's touch?

It was wrong, in so many ways. It was all wrong.

Dedication

To all who know what it feels like to lose a child.

Chapter One

Emma Cook stepped out of her OB-GYN's office Friday afternoon. She slid into her car and pressed her mother's saved number on her cell phone. "Hi, Mom, I just left the doctor."

"Oh, good, honey," she said, relief in her voice. "Your Uncle George called. The meeting with Mark and his lawyer is set for five thirty at Benjamin Industries. Your uncle will meet you there."

She glanced at her watch. "Okay, I should have just enough time to fill the prescription for my pre-natal vitamins."

"I'll let him know." A grin lightened her voice now. "So what did the doctor say?"

"That everything's okay," she said, knowing actually what her mother wanted to hear. "You were right, Mom. You and Steph. He told me what I'm going through is normal and should be over in about six or seven more weeks."

"See, I told you."

Emma growled. "Yes, you did."

"So when are you due?"

She smiled and pressed her hand on her stomach. "Around June twenty-first."

"Close to your father's birthday," she said, softly. "He would've liked that."

Sadness rose, but she pushed it down. "Yes, I think

he would have."

Her mother didn't say anything for a long, thoughtful second. "Look, I'll let you go so you can get to the pharmacy. Don't worry about coming back to work. Steph and I can manage until closing. She just left to help out at her in-laws' anniversary party, but she should be back in an hour or so."

"Mr. and Mrs. Williams like her being there," she said, easing the car toward the exit of the parking lot. She stopped at the road at a sudden memory. "Oh, before I forget, Meg called on Monday. She's got two new clients—big ones—for us. She was supposed to call me back today. If she does, just put the name of the brides on the calendar and I'll take care of the rest."

"Your sister may have gotten that call. Let me check." Her voice faded as she walked through the kitchen area to the office. A few minutes later, she said, "Oh, I see you penciled in the wedding planner's name in June. Looks like Meg hasn't called back yet."

"Okay, Mom." She glanced both ways and then drove out onto the road. "I'm driving now. I'll call you after the meeting to let you know what happened."

"Be careful," she said. "I heard it was supposed to rain again."

"You're kidding."

A quick goodbye was her response. "Love you too, Mom."

She ended the call and threw the phone onto the passenger seat. Emma arrived at the pharmacy ten minutes later and fifteen minutes after that she was on her way to her meeting with the lawyers. Uncle George waved wildly at her when she turned into the large almost empty parking lot. She stopped beside his old dusty truck and slipped out of her small hybrid. Only two other cars shared the lot, both expensive-looking and high-class.

"Wow, you look radiant," George said, holding a large black umbrella over her head. "Pregnancy looks good on you."

She hugged him tight. "I feel better now that I have my vitamins."

"Your mother told me you've been sick." He took her elbow and stepped with her to a side door. "Mr. Benjamin suggested we used this entrance instead of the front door."

"I can only imagine why," she said, sarcasm dripping from her tone. "It certainly wouldn't look right for one of the most respected family court judges to show up at one of the richest families in the area with a pregnant woman, would it?"

He laughed, shaking his head at her statement. "No one can tell Emma."

"No, I'm not fat yet," she said, grinning over at him. "But didn't you just call me radiant."

"You are too much." His grin faded as he tapped her cheek lightly. "I usually don't have to tell my clients this, but... Please let me do the talking. The baby's father thinks he's getting away with something, yet I'm making sure he hurts too."

She narrowed her eyes at him. "I don't want anything from the Benjamins, Uncle George."

"You aren't getting anything," he said, serious judge face replacing his milder uncle one. "That little one he helped to bring into the world is."

"I'm not sure..."

"Don't worry." He patted her hand before reaching

past her to open the door, pressing her into the warm building. He shook the umbrella twice before slamming it shut. "I've taken care of everything for you."

Emma focused on those words as she followed him down the dim hallway toward an open door at the end. He stopped and helped her out of her coat before following her into the conference room. A large table sat in the center of the vast space, with only two chairs on the nearest side. She pulled out one of the chairs from the bare table and sat still until her eyes adjusted to the sharp lighting. Lifting her scrutiny to the two men on the opposite side, she bit her tongue. She frowned at Mark before focusing on the second man. No emotions showed on his lawyer's face—good or bad.

Wow, this would be so much easier if the two men sitting across the table weren't so damn good-looking.

"I'm Lucas Benjamin, Judge Brown." He extended his hand for her uncle's shake. "Does your client understand Mark"—he indicated the frowning man beside him—"is my brother?"

"Yes, his client knows," Emma whispered.

"Good." His deep voice reverberated around the room. "And is that fine with her?"

"It is," she said a bit louder, hands clamped tight in her lap. "I trust my uncle."

"As I do my brother."

Emma refused to look Mark's way.

"Then let's begin." George opened the folder in front of him. He slid a copy of his agreement to the younger lawyer while accepting one from him. Silence lingered in the room while they both looked over the documents. The judge nodded and glanced up at the

4

younger man. "Interesting additions."

"The lawyer I consulted thought they were necessary." Lucas said, the hint of a smile softening his voice. "And you, sir, knew that he would suggest these stipulations."

"Yes."

Emma studied Mark's brother's lowered head through narrowed eyes as he reread the agreement a second time. Dark hair glowed in the sharp lighting, brushing over the top of an expressive suit jacket. The gray material enhanced his wide shoulders while the deep blue tie set off the crisp whiteness of the shirt. He glanced up and focused on her, sending a blast of heat through her system. A quick hint of desire flashed hot in his deep blue eyes, disappearing quickly. Did she just experience that, or was it another strange pregnancy-induced reaction?

Her heart beat inside her chest. Breathe dying tight in her lungs, she forced her look away and glanced at her cupped hands.

Not good, not good at all.

****

What the hell had just happened?

One look at the woman sitting quiet beside the judge slowed his thought-processes and sped up his heart. Even now, seconds after staring at the bright white paper with sharp black lettering, Luke still had a hard time lowering the beat of his heart.

Kathleen had done this to him too. The first time he'd set his eyes on the beautiful blonde ten years ago he'd been just as muddled and confused.

Luke could understand why his brother picked up this woman in the bar. To call her beautiful didn't do

5

her justice.

"Luke, what's wrong?"

He closed his eyes for a moment and then moved his hand toward his brother. "I'm just reading through the agreement, Mark."

Mark growled loud. "How many times do you need to read it? Just give it to me so I can sign the damn thing and get out of here. Rebecca will be here any minute. I want this over and done with before she gets here."

He fought his temper at his brother's cold attitude. Sometimes he could be a total ass. Pushing away the thought, he rubbed his eyes and placed his hands flat on the table on both sides of the paper.

"Are we in agreement, Mr. Benjamin?"

The air still sizzled around Luke when he glanced up at the older man, attempting to ignore the sexy lady sitting beside him. He swallowed dryness and picked up the page, studying the document word by word until his mind could once again understand it. That's when he noticed the new dollar amount—double what he agreed to at their earlier meeting.

"It seems I'm not the only one changing our tentative agreement."

Judge Brown grinned. "That is because I knew the lawyer friend you consulted would insist on the paternity test and that the child be over eighteen before receiving any of the trust fund money. I was expecting—"

The woman sat up straight and glared at her lawyer, as if only now hearing the stipulations added to his document. She glared at her lawyer before turning it full-force on him and then his brother. "You bastard."

"Emma, that's enough," the older man whispered. "I expected these changes."

"You expected…"

Her chest expanded in and out as she fought her anger, pressing the sweet mounds of her breasts into the smooth, light fabric of her blouse. He forced back the unexpected reaction to her unintended sexiness. A foot slammed into his outer thigh. His brother's suggestive wink and grin erupted hot in him.

"…but he's calling me a liar, Uncle George."

Her low moan-like whisper settled on his damaged heart, soothing over it in a warm wash of hopefulness. Kathleen's death had torn him up, wounding him for another chance. Two and a half years ago, he'd infuriated her so much she'd gotten into the car and drove away. January snow had been falling hard that morning, making driving bad for normally functioning individuals. His crying wife didn't have a chance. A police officer's arrival at the office a few hours later told him of his loss. His heart had been as dead and icy as that cold January day since.

And, with one look, the woman who carried his brother's baby found a way to start the healing.

Without even being aware he needed it.

"No, I won't agree to that." Emma yelled out her statement this time, no soft, healing whispers now. "If that's what I need to agree to," she said, grabbing up the paper and crushing it in her hand. "Then I refuse to sign anything."

"Emmie, be reasonable," the older man said, pulling the paper from her trembling hands. "Don't you think he has the right to know for sure the baby is his?"

"You mean, the sperm donor," she said, glaring

hard at his silent brother. "Because a *father* wouldn't insist his baby's mother *take care of it*."

His brother had the dignity to look down.

"Like I'm going to kill my child," she said, standing up from her seat and leaning over the table. "You are not worth it, Mark."

"I didn't tell…"

She leaned in even closer, pushing the table hard into his direction. "No, you didn't say the words. But what was I supposed to think?"

"Emmie, sit down."

The judge's calming voice pulled her hot look from his brother to him for a disturbing second before she sighed and fell back into her seat. She tapped her nails quick against the table top. "So how will this work? How will he know when I have the baby if he's not allowed to come near me?" Her hand slammed flat in a harsh, final way. "And, he will not be allowed anywhere near me or my family."

Luke nodded. "That's the deal, Ms. Cook."

She refused to look up at him. "Then how will he know?"

He looked at the judge and then back at the calmer woman. "Your uncle will let me know and I'll make arrangements with a private lab to have the test done."

"And no names will be given to this lab?"

"None," he said, forcing his professionalism to the forefront of his brain. "The laboratory we'll be working with is a discreet, trustworthy facility."

She did look up then, eyes narrowed at his comment. His throat tightened at the intensity, heat rushing throughout his body. Yet he sensed his professional expression and demeanor on the outside didn't show the riot of emotions blasting inside him. He was aware enough to keep his thoughts buried.

"You'll guarantee it?"

"Yes."

"Okay." She snatched the paper from Judge Brown's hand and skimmed the agreement once again before signing her name to the bottom of it. "There."

"And there," Mark said, pressing the document he'd signed to Emma and snatching at hers. After signing the second one, he set the pen down and stood up. "I'm glad that's finally over."

Luke clamped his hands into fist, fighting his anger. "Yes, it's over, Mark."

His brother stopped near the doorway and faced him.

"This is the last time," he said, gathering up the signed agreement and placing it into his folder. He would have Dan make copies of it and send it on to the judge later. "Next time you get into a jam, you're on your own."

His brother narrowed his eyes for a second in confusion before a grin erupted. "Like I haven't heard that before."

Luke hit the folder on the table. "I'm serious, Mark."

His brother froze at his subdued anger before snorting and walking out the doorway.

"You did the right thing, son." The judge pushed back his chair and stood. "Send me copies of your agreement for Emma and my files, and I'll do the same."

"I will do that, Judge."

The older man nodded as he collected his folder

and coat. The door closed soft behind him at his exit. He pressed his seat back and glanced across the table.

"My uncle is right, Mr. Benjamin."

"Luke," he said, surprising her with his sign of friendship. Why he wasn't letting her go was beyond him. Nothing good could come from getting to know this woman better. "My first name is Luke."

Her eyes widened before she smiled gently. "My name is Emma."

"Emma," he said, loving the sound of the name. "What actually was your uncle right about?"

"That it's time you stopped getting that…brother of yours out of bad situations," she whispered, gaze tracing heated interest over his face. "Mark doesn't look anything like you."

He swallowed and stayed quiet as she spread that penetrating look down his body and then up again. Like with a touch of real fingers, he reacted in a real way. Thankfully the table blocked his lower body from her view. He sighed when she finally focused onto his heated face again. A sweet, slight flush warmed her cheeks for a brief moment.

Damn, why did this woman have to make him start feeling? Why did the woman carrying his brother's child make him aware of how long it'd been since he felt a female's touch?

It was wrong, in so many ways. It was all wrong.

"Do you look like your father or mother?"

Her innocent question pulled his mind off his dilemma. "I'm not sure."

"You're not sure?" She sat forward for a moment before slipping onto her feet. "I look more like my mother; my sister looks like my Dad."

"I'm adopted," he whispered, glancing down at the table. "So were my two younger sisters."

"So that's why you think you need to fix all of Mark's problems?"

"Not just his." No anger or pain roared in him at her question. "I'm the firm's lawyer, so I help everyone here."

"Oh, really?" Emma placed her hands on the table and leaned toward him, a real smile playing around her mouth. "I bet Mark's your best client."

"How did you guess that?" Her smile deepened, wrapping around his emotions with total ease. God, but he loved her smile. And her voice. A part of him wanted to sit down and close his eyes, so he could feel that soft, sensual voice weave around him. He'd been alone too long. "You're right, though."

She studied him as he picked up his briefcase from the chair and slipped the forgotten folder inside it. He pulled his coat from the back of the chair and slipped his arms into the sleeves.

"I guess that means it's time to go," she said, a cross between anger and understanding lowering her voice. "Before I do…" She searched around the room, settling on something behind his left shoulder. "Is that a bathroom?"

"Yes." Puzzled by the unexpected question, understanding hit him when her hand slid down the flatness of her stomach. "Oh?" He twisted to his side and waved past him. "I'll wait until you're finished."

"Thank you."

The door swung shut a second before a loud bang echoed near him. He jerked toward the sound and stared at the person entering the conference room. Drops of wetness flew into him as Rebecca swished her wet hair around her face. "It's pouring out there again."

"Rebecca, what are you doing here?"

"Oh, I'm sorry." She pressed against the door to keep it tight to the wall. "I don't know why this thing slams into the wall every time I open it." She lifted her hand and looked at the door for a long second. "Stay, door."

He couldn't help but smile at her expression. "I think you're just trying to scare me, like you used to do when we were kids."

"Did it work?"

"No," he said, forcing his grin away. She needed to leave before Emma finished in the bathroom. "Mark's not here."

"I can see that." She backed from the door toward the table. "He just called me and told me he's going to his office. It's pouring outside so I decided to check the side door and it opened. Then I noticed the light on here. I didn't think this room was ever used."

"Only for special meetings." The toilet flushed, freezing him in his steps. He needed to get her out of here—now. "I'm on my way to my dad's office. I can take you to Mark, if you'd like. That way you won't have to go back outside in the rain."

"No, that's okay," Rebecca said. "I know how to get there from here."

The door squealed open, causing his friend to look in Emma's direction. She stood straighter and then winked at him. "Well, Luke, do you have something to tell me?"

"No." Nothing showed in her stance or her eyes when she gazed his way. He shrugged and looked back at Rebecca. "I don't have anything to tell you."

"Oh, really?" She glanced at Emma and then back at him. "I think Kathleen would be happy you finally found someone."

"What?" Emma said.

"Found someone?" His reply erased hers. "No, you've got it all wrong."

Chapter Two

The sly look narrowing in the woman's eyes backed Emma up a few steps. She blinked and then peeked at the silent, controlled man near her. "Luke and I—"

"Look Rebecca," the man said at the same time, stealing an apologetic look her way. "Emma and I are...friends."

Friends? What is the man talking about? All Luke was to her was the lawyer who represented the asshole who got her pregnant, and all she was to him was someone to force out of his brother's life. It didn't matter if she had no intention of making the man do the right thing. The lawyer thought it necessary to make her sign a stupid agreement—two agreements—so his brother would be free of his responsibility.

"So how long have you known each other?" Luke's friend asked. "I don't remember Mark mentioning you were dating—"

"I'm not dating him." Emma stepped closer to her. "I was dating his—"

"Hey, Emmie, give it up." His stiff arm wrapped around her waist, his hand settling light into the curve of her hip. "Rebecca found out, so..."

She froze in place, yet he didn't drop his arm from her. Instead he bumped her hip in a gentle way, sending a hot rush of fire through her system. She lost her breath for a second before gasping one in loud, fighting the unexpected shivers traveling over her arms. What was wrong with her? Why was she allowing this man to manhandle her like his brother used to do? Why wasn't she jerking away from him?

"Wow, I'm glad you found someone, Luke." Rebecca stepped in front of her. "Even though I've no idea what her name is." She mocked glared at Luke. "I'm a bit hurt you didn't tell me."

Before she could stop the words, Emma said, "My name is Emma Cook."

"Emma is such a pretty—" Her bright blue eyes widened at the same time as her mouth spread opened in astonishment. "Cook? Are you a part of the catering company?"

She glanced at Luke and then nodded. "My family owns it. I manage the office. My mother and younger sister take care of the cooking and baking."

"Oh, wow."

The woman's reaction shook her. "Why?"

"My wedding planner, Meg, just called to tell me she secured my wedding date in August with your company."

"Emma is your caterer?"

Something in the man's voice tore her eyes off the other woman and onto him. He looked worried, upset. But why?

"Yes," Rebecca said. "Meg told me they—" She pointed toward her. "That they were the best in the area."

Emma was proud of that.

"Yet for some reason Mark wasn't happy about it," she said, placing her hand on the top of the chair. "I got him to change his mind, though."

"Mark?" The arm around her waist tightened, fingers spreading over the left side of her stomach. She pushed away from him. "Your brother?"

Luke nodded.

"No." Now she understood why he was holding her this way. Once again he was protecting his asshole of a brother. "No."

Joyful laughter rang through the room. "Oh, looks like your lady knows my man."

"Oh, you can say that?" Long, smooth fingers pressed hard into her stomach, stopping her from voicing what she thought of her *man*. She twisted her head toward Luke, catching a pleading look in his eyes. "Oh, I can't talk about him."

A musical sound rang in the room. Rebecca pulled a cell from her open coat pocket and grinned. "Oops, speaking of Mark." She twisted away from them and answered it. "Hey, honey."

Luke shook his head, a cross between remorse and imploring burning in his eyes. Emma leaned as far from him as his still tight hold would allow and studied his conflicting expression. Her temper flared hot inside at his action, burning up into her throat. "Still fixing things for him?"

The blue of his eyes darkened almost black before he sighed and gentled his fingers down her cheek, pressing a lock of her shoulder-length hair away from her face. Her skin tingled under his touch. The corner of his mouth lowered into a slight frown, eyes widening in stunned disbelief. He traced his finger lightly to her chin.

"Yeah, you two are just…friends."

It took everything in her to pull her gaze from the man, yet she finally managed it. Rebecca stepped into her line of sight, friendly look focused on her. "Luke has been alone for two and a half years, did he tell you that?"

She shook her head.

Her smile widened. "I was about ready to start introducing him to some of my friends."

"Oh?"

"Looks like I won't need to now." She placed her phone into her pocket and zipped her coat. "Mark is waiting for me in his office so I'll leave you two alone."

"Rebecca, Emma and I are only friends," Luke said, an urgent plea deepening his tone. "Maybe someday we'll be more, but not yet."

Only friends? Someday maybe we'll be more? Panic shook her at the wrongness of this whole situation. Emma pulled away from his loosening arms and slide past the surprised shorter woman. Luke called her name. She ignored him.

Ice-cold wetness dampened her blouse when she raced from the building to her car, forcing her to tighten her arms around her middle. Beating rain flowed down her cheeks, chilling her face in a blast of bitter October wind. She wiped hard at her eyes and looked at her tiny car, sitting alone in the empty parking lot. Alone like she felt now, alone and foolish for thinking this man was any different than his asshole brother. Emptiness erupted deep into her. Pain.

"Emma?"

She wiped the raindrops away. Or were they tears? "Leave me alone."

"Here's your coat," he said, opening it for her.

"You'll freeze."

As if out of her control, she raised her arms and allowed him to slip it onto her body. She grabbed the edges and tightened it around her. "Thank you."

"You need to get in your car."

"Yes," she said, seeing no reason to deny the obvious. "But it's not your problem."

"I...had to do it."

"Yes." She jerked the few steps to her door, found her keys and unlocked it. Slipping inside, she shut the door on the now crouching man. Rain dinged hard on the rooftop. "You had your say. Now just leave me be."

His coat opened in the rainy wind, plastering the pristine white dress shirt tight to his chest. Emma tore her look from it to his face, clamping her hands into fist. Even wet this man looked too fine.

"Wait here."

Emma shook her head, but didn't place the key into the ignition.

"The weather is crazy," he said, tapping on the window to get her attention. He pointed in the direction of the other cars. "I'll get my car and follow you home."

"No."

"Emma, please."

The pleading was back in his voice, the guilt. A blurry vision wavered near her window a second as her eyes filled with tears again. She needed to start her car and drive away, yet her hands refused to move the key to the ignition. He was the enemy, even though he acted as if he truly wanted to be a friend.

"Give me a minute, Emma."

He disappeared out of view. She closed her eyes,

taking in a couple of deep breaths. A powerful engine roared in the sudden silence of the wind, and then a horn blared. She jerked her head up and her key into the ignition, starting her vehicle and following the dark car to the main road. He pulled to the side and slowed, allowing her to drive past.

Rain pounded the windshield with a ferocity that matched her troubled emotions. She clamped her hands around the wheel at the two and the ten positions, keeping her tear-filled eyes focused on the brake lights of the car in front of her. Sooner than she thought possible considering the weather and her turmoil, she reached the exit and turned off the freeway. The wheels hydroplaned slightly off the road, startling out a breath. She righted the vehicle and sped up.

Minutes later, Emma turned into the driveway of her one-story home. Her tears had stopped falling, eyesight was clearer, yet she still only saw that paper she'd signed. That paper that was now void because of Luke's action.

"Emma, you're going to freeze."

If she froze out here, wouldn't that solve her problem? No baby, no fake boyfriend, no catering job for the fiancé of—

"No."

"Emma?"

What was wrong with her? She clutched the keys tight in her hands and gripped at the door knob, opening it so quickly Luke had to step back. She slipped out of the car, locked it and moved toward her front door. She left it open for Luke. It closed with a click behind her and then silence filled the room.

"You just messed everything up." His continued

quiet caused her to face him. "Uncle George isn't going to be pleased."

A lop-sided grin broke over his sullen face. "Neither is my brother."

Shouldn't she be angry with him? Yet, instead of a heated response, her shoulders sagged in defeat. Rarely in her life, had she been so unsure of what to do. "All I wanted was to be free of your brother. That's all."

"You are free, Emma."

"Am I?" She studied him for a quick moment. "I don't think so. Not now. How can I be free of him if I'm catering his wedding?" She glared at him, shoulders squared in a brief burst of anger. It left as quickly as it'd arrived. "How can I be free when you just implied to that same woman that we are more than friends?"

Chapter Three

Luke stayed silent, letting her speak her mind. Her green eyes glistened in the brightness of the overhead light, cheeks slightly wet with a trace of tears and rain. A part of him wanted to wipe off her cheek, a part he'd buried deep when his Kathleen died. He wanted to bury it back down, yet he couldn't do it. The pain of that time settled hard on his heart, threatening to overwhelm him.

"You don't have anything to say, Mr. Benjamin?"

Strength echoed in that question, a hint of sarcasm. He'd just met her a few hours ago and yet he sensed this was her usual way of handling problems. He pushed the painful memories aside and focused on the woman. He needed to find distance from both—the past and the presence. He needed time to think through why he'd hugged her to his side. Instead of leaving, he said, "I could use a cup of coffee."

"What?" A slight confusion sounded in her tone. "Coffee? You want coffee?"

He nodded, and waved his hand in her direction. "We need to talk, so we might as well have some coffee."

She studied him and then shrugged. "Sure."

Whatever emotion had gotten hold of her in the conference room seemed to be gone now. And he breathed a sigh of relief. Now he'll have a few minutes to figure out why he'd put both of them in this strange situation. Yes, it did keep her from hinting about the real reason the two of them were in that particular room. And it did help out the Benjamin family and business temporarily. Since he'd graduated law school, he'd been working to keep his adopted family in a good light. Yet was that the only motivation for acting like Emma was more than his friend?

"Are you hungry?"

His body jerked into life at her innocent question, blood flowing down into his cock. He twisted away from her at his reaction. What the hell is wrong with him? Even Kathleen hadn't gotten him so hard, so easily, with just a simple innocent question. His brother was the one who did things without thinking first, not him.

"Mr. Benjamin?"

Idiot. He was acting the fool. Nothing good could come from him getting involved with the woman his brother had gotten pregnant. Nothing.

"Luke?"

So why in the hell didn't he just leave? Why the hell was he following her into the kitchen?

"Well, I am," she whispered.

Light footsteps moved across the tiled floor a second before the refrigerator opened. He took in a few deep breaths, and looked toward her. And he lost his new-found focus all over again at the sight. She bent over further and pulled out a large covered dish, righting to her full height before he forced his eyes to the closing refrigerator door.

Shit.

"Do you like lasagna?" She carried the dish to the

stove and set it down. "My aunt cooked it for me."

"Oh?" Guess the blood still hadn't made it back to his brain yet. "I...could eat something."

"Lasagna?"

"Sure," he said, shaking the last of the inappropriate thoughts. She turned on the stove before stepping to the coffeepot. A few second later brown liquid steamed into the glass carafe. He sniffed in the rich scent. "Do you need any help?"

"No, I've got it." She didn't look his way. "Just sit down, okay?"

The man in him stayed stubbornly on his feet. Maybe Mark was an asshole when it came to women, but he wasn't the same. It was important she saw the difference between them. "I would rather help you, Emma."

She did look his way then, a sweet grin lifting her mouth. "That's kind of you, Luke, but I'm fine."

Luke relaxed under her smile, yet he still didn't sit down. Instead he stepped toward the refrigerator, opened it, and searched through it. Covered dish after dish sat on the two main shelves, with milk and a half-gallon of orange juice on the side with the usual condiments. She said his name. He ignored her as he bent and pulled out the crisper drawer. Snatching a bag of lettuce, some cherry tomatoes, an onion, and a cucumber, he set them on the counter and faced her. A cross between confusion and a hint of anger made him grin as he kicked the door closed.

Emma narrowed her eyes, and then shrugged. "If you insist on helping, you'll find a big bowl in that cabinet." She pointed to a lower cabinet next to the refrigerator. She took a small knife from the block near the stove and a forked-spoon from the drawer under it. "Here."

The coffee machine gurgled. He made the salad and dressing with ingredients she placed near him, setting the bowls on the table for her. She slid the lasagna into the oven, set the table, and poured the coffee. Garlic and tomato scents waved through the room, making his stomach growl in anticipation.

"I love Aunt Cora's Italian." Emma took a small sip of her coffee. "I love my mother and Aunt Helen's cooking too, but Italian is my favorite." She grinned around her cup. "But that's our little secret."

His heart sped. "Your secret is safe with me."

A frown lowered her grin for a moment. "No, I'm not going to think about anything that happened today."

"Good," he said, picking up his cup and sipping. The smooth, rich taste of the coffee pleased his tongue. "I'd much rather enjoy your Aunt Cora's delicious smelling lasagna."

A comfortable quietness settled around him. Mark had mentioned she was good-looking, but his description didn't do her justice. Soft reddish-brown hair slipped against her cheek and bright green eyes shined warm at him. His breath stopped tight in his lungs when she chuckled and focused a playful look onto him.

"I can see why my brother—" He waved his hand toward her. "Forget I mentioned his name, I know how he upsets you."

Emma glanced down at her cup and then back up at him. No expression showed in her face. "I really didn't want anything from your brother, Luke."

"I believe you," he said, hearing the truth in her

simple statement. "The lawyer friend I consulted told me that Judge Brown would change the amount we agreed on when we talked a few days ago. And that I needed to make it clear the money was meant for the child only. That's why my friend suggested I add the need for both a paternity test and set a minimum age requirement for the child. "

"I don't want any of his money."

He heard the truth in her adamant statement.

"And it's Mark's baby," she said, softly. "The only other man I slept with in the last decade was my ex-husband."

His head shoot up at her admission. "Really?"

A hint of anger flashed across her face before she took a loud breath and let it out slowly. "I had a reason for acting the way I did that night. A personal reason that's none of your business."

Luke nodded. "I understand."

"Do you?"

He should feel guilty for what he did suspect was her motive for sleeping with his brother. His legal assistant's research on Emma and her business was thorough, even the more personal stuff about her attempt at having a baby. Well, he wasn't sure of that. But why else would a couple go to a special fertility doctor?

"So your brother's fiancée is really an old friend of yours?"

"Yes." Thankfully she changed the conversation to a safer one. "Rebecca and I have been friends since grade school."

"That long?"

He grinned. "She was the first person I met when I

started school here, after my adoption was final."

"Oh, that's sweet." She picked up her coffee and took a sip. "So what happened?"

"What do you mean?"

The timer rang out before he could get his answer. He stood from his seat but Emma waved him back down and wandered to the stove, shutting it off and pulling the dish out of the oven. He picked up the plates and walked toward her, holding one then the other out for a heaping helping of the hot, mozzarella dripping meal. His mouth watered at the enjoyable sight and pleasing scent, his stomach growl loud in the quiet room.

"Guess you are hungry?" A chuckle warmed the air. "It tastes as good as it looks and smells. Just wait."

"I believe you." He set the plates in place and waited for Emma to sit before he settled into his seat. Reaching for his fork, he stopped the movement and watched Emma fill her smaller plate with a mound of salad and handed him the bowl. He dished out salad, dousing his greens with Italian dressing. Then he picked up his fork and dug into the hot meal. "Well, here goes."

"You'll like it." She stabbed at a cherry tomato. "All the women in my family can cook. Well, most of them."

An explosion of flavor touched his mouth: garlic and tomato and the heated stretch of the mild cheese mixed with the spices and herbs in the meat. He grinned her way and took another bite. "Wow, you're right. This is great. No wonder Cook's is the best caterer in the area."

"Thanks."

Her face flushed warm with pleasure, shoulders relaxing against her seat. Luke let out a breath as he cut another bite. She acted and sounded much better, emotions more under control. "So which aunt can't cook?"

"Aunt?" She lowered her fork for a second. "Oh, you're wondering which Cook female can't even boil water?"

He nodded around another bite of lasagna.

"That would be me," she said, piercing her fork into the greens. "I didn't inherit the cooking gene."

"Cooking gene?"

She shrugged. "My sister Stephanie got that."

"You can't cook at all?"

Emma grinned, and pointed toward the refrigerator. "All of that stuff in there is from my Mom and aunts." She chased after another small tomato before catching it with her fork. "It makes sense, though. Every time my sister and I visited the shop, I always ended up in the office with my father. Steph spent all her time in the kitchen. We spend more time there and at school than we did home."

"So you run the place with your dad now?"

Sadness darkened her eyes, a flash of wetness winking in the overhead lights. "Dad...died, almost a year ago."

Luke jerked up in surprise. His assistant never told him anything about her father's death. "Oh, I'm sorry."

"I...miss him." She swallowed down her agony and straightened up. "It was his heart. One day it just gave out on him."

He didn't know what to say, so he just touched her arm. She froze for a moment before placing her hand on top of his. "Thank you."

And it felt so right. Being with this woman exposed something deep inside him, bringing it to the surface. He hadn't enjoyed just talking to a woman in a long time, since Kathleen's death. Coldness washed over his hand when she moved hers away, and he buried the feeling back down. Emma was the wrong woman for him in so many ways. Getting too involved with her would be a major mistake.

"Want more lasagna?"

He did. But not because he was still hungry. It was because if he kept eating, he wouldn't have to leave. Luke didn't want to leave her.

She laughed. "Even though you already went back for seconds a while ago."

"It's good." He placed his fork on the plate and pushed it from him. "Thank you." He took a sip of the warm liquid and glanced at his watch. "What?" He reread the time and frowned. "It's nine."

"No, it can't be—" Emma glanced behind him at the big kitchen clock on the wall. "Wow, you're right." Her eyes widened in disbelief. "How could so much time go by without either of us noticing?"

Shit, this wasn't good either. This same thing happened when he first started dating Kathleen. Time stood still whenever they were together. He shook that thought away and stood from his chair. "I need to get going."

Emma opened her mouth, closed it and nodded. "That's probably a good idea."

She preceded him out of the kitchen into the dim living room and stopped at the front door. He took his coat from a chair near the door and put it on, gathering his keys in his hands.

Why was he having such a hard time leaving?

"Thank you, Luke," Emma whispered, spreading her arms around her middle. "For…everything."

"You're welcome." He stopped at the door, hand on the knob. *Leave, Benjamin. Now.* "Are you feeling better?"

"Yes." She dropped her arms from her middle and stepped closer to him. "Will your friend… Will Rebecca tell anyone what she saw earlier?"

Hopefully not, yet Luke couldn't be sure. "Rebecca is usually a good person to tell secrets too, but…"

"Yet she wouldn't think you having a new relationship would be a secret, would she?"

God, what have I done? He had no reason to hug her so tight to his side. He only did it because he suddenly needed to know what she would feel like against him. Rebecca's arrival gave him that chance. A fucking selfish act on his part.

"Oh, why did I meet your brother at the bar that night instead of you?"

Her soft whisper roared in the intense quiet, slamming hard into his chest. She sighed and stepped backward toward the arm of the couch. He moved forward and placed his hand on her warm cheek, tracing his fingers over the softness of her chin and neck. Her eyes closed slowly, lips parting. His mouth dropped to hers in urgent need.

"No," he said roughly, yanking his mouth from hers. He stepped away. "I need to go, Emma."

"Yes."

Disappointment and guilt burned from her eyes. She lowered her head for a moment, and when she looked up again, he read nothing good in her gaze.

Just sadness, just emptiness.

Just the same type of thing he was feeling right now.

"Goodbye, Luke."

Everything about this woman was wrong for him, yet he was determined this not be the end. He touched her cheek lightly, placing his finger under her chin and lifting her head. "I want to see you again, Emma."

The sadness deepened in her eyes. "We can't, Luke."

If he was going to act the fool, might as well go all the way. "I wish I'd meet you at the bar too, Emma."

"Luke?"

"I'll call you tomorrow."

He opened the door and stepped outside, closing it behind him.

And stopped, waiting to see what she would do.

Leave, Benjamin. Things were too confusing now, for both of them. Neither of them had even noticed that it'd stopped raining. Or maybe she had, but he definitely hadn't. He needed to leave so he could find the time to think through his action.

Taking that first step to his car was the hardest thing he had done in a long time.

Chapter Four

"Is Dr. Greenlee available to speak to me yet?"

"She's still busy, Mr. Benjamin," the receptionist said. "I told her you needed to talk with her."

Luke sighed. Why did Rebecca have to be so busy? "Tell her I need her to call back as soon as possible, okay? It's important."

"I'll remind her of your call again."

"Thank you." He said goodbye and ended the call. *Please call me Rebecca.*

Luke set the phone in its charging cradle and moved to the window. A light rain fell against it, sliding down the glass in shining wetness. He'd been trying to get in touch with Rebecca all weekend, leaving her message after message at home and now at her office. So far no one had hinted about him being in a new relationship, yet that didn't mean anything. He'd been busy in his office. Except for a quick run to the breakroom around lunch time, he'd been alone. Even his assistant had stayed at his desk all morning.

His phone buzzed, sending his hand jerking toward it. *Please be you, Rebecca.* "Benjamin Industries."

"Luke?"

Shit. "Mark, I don't have time to talk now. I'm waiting on a call."

His brother laughed. "When aren't you?"

"What do you want?" Experience told him his

31

brother wouldn't end the call until he had his say. "Is everything going okay at the Columbus restaurant? Dad told me you had some problem over the weekend."

"Oh, I've settled that," he said. "Work is fine. What I need to ask is if Rebecca saw Emma Friday night."

"Emma?"

"Yes, did she see her?" Anxiety rode harsh in his words. "Rebecca told me she stopped in the conference room on the way to my office. She said you were there."

But what else did she tell you? "I was there, yes."

"Was Emma?"

"Yes, but she was in the bathroom."

"So Rebecca didn't see her?"

"No, she was looking for you." It didn't sit well lying. Untruthfulness at any time made him uneasy. "You want some advice, Mark." He didn't give his brother time to say yes or no. "Instead of worrying about your lady finding out, why not just confess your sin to her?"

A harsh growl roared out of the line. "Are you fucking crazy? Rebecca would leave me forever if she found out I got another woman pregnant."

He clamped his hand hard around the phone. "Don't you think she deserves to know the truth?"

Mark laughed. "Why? You and that judge fixed things for me. Other than depositing that money into a trust fund for the kid and giving blood for that test, I'm free of it."

Shit, his brother could be a total asshole.

"I just wanted to know if Rebecca and Emma talked, that's all."

He should just tell the truth. Why the hell did he cover for his brother all the time? "No, Emma was in the bathroom."

"Good." Relief sounded clear in the phone. "Now if only I can convince her to use another caterer for the wedding. Gotta go, little brother."

He glared at the phone for a second and then replaced it in the base. His reflection in the window showed his sarcastic grin. Did he even know his fiancée? "I doubt even you could change her mind."

Maybe he should hint to Rebecca not all is well, but that would only hurt his old friend. She truly loved that asshole brother of his, had since she returned home from college before going on to medical school. At the time, Mark cared about her too. Yet now Luke wasn't so sure of that. Would a man who loved someone continue to sleep with another woman? Maybe once, yes, because he had a weak moment. Not a dozen or so times afterward.

And it hadn't been the first time. Benjamin Industries had paid a few other women to stay silent because of his brother's inability to remember he was engaged.

Why do you stay with him, Rebecca?

The phone buzzing on his desk stopped his contemplation and he turned to pick it up. "Benjamin Industries."

"Hey, Luke," Rebecca said. "Sorry it's taken me so long to get back with you, but it's been busy the last few days."

"I'm glad you finally called." Relief sank him into his seat. "I won't take up much of your time. I just need to ask a favor."

"Sure," she said, letting out a breath. "Anything."

"It's about…" He hesitated, unsure how to word his request. Did it really matter what words he used with his friend? She already suspected something was up, something that involved Emma. Unfortunately, her suspicious were all wrong. "It's about…Emma."

"Emma?" She went silent for a second, then she said. "Oh, you mean Emma Cook, your new lady."

"We're only friends, Rebecca."

"Sure, you are," she said, with a joyful laugh. "But I'll let you believe what you want to believe now, I'm too busy."

"Thanks." Before she could make another comment, he said, "Could you hold off telling anyone about her?"

Silence filtered in the line again. "Why, Luke? She seems like a nice woman."

"She is." He jerked straight at his instantaneous agreement. "Everything is so…new for us. And I just found out she dated…someone I know. It'll be a little uncomfortable for her." Hopefully he hadn't said anything to give his brother away. If anyone was going to cause Rebecca pain, it wouldn't be him. "And I'd rather get to know her better before Mom and Dad find out."

"Yes, especially your mom." Joyful laughter blasted into his ear. "She thinks two and half years is plenty of time to get over Kathleen too."

So did his dad. But his mother was more vocal about her beliefs, speaking of them every time he talked with her. He loved his mother, yet her attitude was getting to him. Could her attitude be a reason for his action yesterday with Emma? Could her and his sisters' veiled threats to introduce him to some of their friends be the reason for his unthoughtful action?

"You know I can't keep a secret well, Luke," Rebecca said. "But I'll try." Another voice rose in the line. "Look, I have to get going. I think one of my mamas-to-be is ready to deliver."

The call ended then, and the contradiction in the whole bizarre situation came to sudden light. Why it only hit him now he didn't understand, yet it was ironic all the same.

Rebecca was one of the best OB/GYNs in the area.

Wouldn't it be poetic justice if Emma selected her as her doctor?

****

"Emma, you ready to go?" Her mother peeked around the door before stepping into her office. "Steph and I are getting something to eat at the diner tonight. It's been such a busy week, we're thinking of treating ourselves. Are you up for that, or are you too tired?"

"It is Saturday night, so why not?" Emma grinned at her mother. "I just have a few more things to do before I can leave."

"Okay, I'll wait here for you." She moved into the office and settled in one of the chairs with a long sigh. "Feels good to sit down for a bit."

"Oh?" Emma took her focus off the Excel form. "You went with Steph and the servers to the Fitzgerald anniversary party?"

Her mother nodded. "Zora didn't show up again."

Emma leaned back into her seat and sighed. "This is... What? Two times this week?"

"Three." Her mother frowned. "I'm thinking we have to let her go."

"Won't be easy." She groaned. "You know she's going to cry racism, if we let her go."

"I know." Her mother nodded. "But don't worry, I've got witnesses and proof for every incident. Her lawyer father can try to sue us like he did the last place she worked, but it won't work."

"Good," she said, refocusing on her form for a moment before saving it. "Want to hear some good news?" She shut down the computer and pushed back her seat. "Every Friday, Saturday, and Sunday in June is filled with catering jobs, and five days in July and three in August."

"Really? Already?"

Emma laughed. "We even have a couple of weddings to cater in late May and early September."

"Nice to be so popular, isn't it?" Her mother stood from her chair and lifted her arms high over her head. "Tiring, but good. Your father would be pleased."

An image of her dad rose in her mind, the way he looked right after he'd negotiated a big deal. A mixture of pride and arrogance washed over his face, enhanced by a big grin and a wink toward her. Of all the time she spent alone with her dad growing up, those times were the best. She'd been proud to be his daughter.

"You ready, honey?"

She shook the feeling away and slipped from her seat. Making sure everything was locked down she turned off the light and followed her mother out toward the customer area. "I'm ready."

"About time," her mother said, with a grin. "I'm starving for my usual onion rings and BLT."

"I'll have a chicken salad sandwich." Emma laughed. "That's about the only thing I can stomach nowadays."

Her mother tapped her back. "Give it time, Em. You've been taking pre-natal vitamins for the last week, right? And they're helping. You'll be able to eat better soon."

"Is she complaining again?" Her sister stood at the front door, clad in coat, gloves, and hat, holding out a coat in each hand. She handed one to their mother and then turned to Emma. "Here you go. It finally stopped raining, but now it's cold. Be glad when the weather gets back to normal. The last few weeks have been outrageous."

"I heard it's supposed to warm up soon." Emma put on and zipped up her garment. She let go of her sister's complaint about the weather and focused on her question. "Mom was promising me that the morning sickness would end."

Steph sniffed. "What a complainer."

"Like I'm the only one who complains?"

Her sister shrugged. "At least I believe the weather guy."

"Your big sister will just have to live with it," her mother said, wrapping her arms around both of their waists. She hugged them tight to her sides. "Now, let's go. I'm starving."

Emma looked at Steph and then grinned as her mother walked to her car. "Does she ever eat any of her own stuff?"

Steph shook her head. "You know Mom."

Yes, she knew her mother well. She was honest to the core. Her parents were both that way, teaching her and her sister the right way to do business. Emma always suspected it was the company's internal values of honesty, caring, and good quality that made them so popular with everyone.

Like with Rebecca.

Her mind drifted back to the moment she walked out of the bathroom a week ago and spotted the elegant, well-dressed blonde woman standing near Luke. She looked vaguely familiar but she hadn't recognized her from the newspaper article. Not until she mentioned Meg's name and getting Cooks to do her wedding. Then she'd just freaked out, and completely, totally lost it.

A week had gone by since she found out Cooks would be catering her wedding, and she still had a hard time accepting it. She was surprised her uncle hadn't found out about it yet. But then Luke had his own reasons for keeping it from him. She pressed her fingers to her lips and sighed. It was a simple little kiss so why was it still affecting her?

Damn.

"You okay, Emma?" Steph set the alarm and locked the shop. "You've been acting stranger than normal lately."

"I'm fine."

"If you say so," her sister said, moving past her toward their mother. "Let's go. I'm looking forward to my once a week burger with the works and fries."

Emma stepped beside her sister and wandered down the street to the busy diner. Maybe there was a way Cooks could get out of catering that August wedding. "Mom, could I ask you something?"

"Honey?"

She moved to walk with her mother, leaving her sister alone behind them. "Has Dad ever changed his mind about catering a wedding?"

"What?" Her mother glanced at her but didn't stop until she reached the edge of the curb at the side street. "Why are you asking?"

"I mean, after he'd given the wedding planner or whoever his okay." Emma stepped away from her mother. "Did he ever change his mind?"

"No. Never. Why?"

"I'm thinking we might have to say no to one of our newest brides," she said, stepping from the sidewalk onto the road. She didn't say another word until she stood outside the small diner. "Here we are."

"Emma," her sister said, setting her hand on her shoulder. "Finish your thought."

She glanced at her frown, and then sighed. "One of our newest jobs…Rebecca Greenlee is Mark's fiancée."

Both her mother and sister stood straight, focusing wide eyes on her. Her mother shook her head. "Are you serious?"

"Luke told me last week at the conference with Judge Brown and the sperm donor."

"Honey…language."

"Well, it's true." Emma glanced at her silent sister. "A few days before that Meg called and said she had two big weddings for us—one in June and one in August. Rebecca's and the sperm—Mark's is the one in August. She hadn't confirmed either date until the day before yesterday, though. That's why I didn't say anything until now. I was hoping she would change her mind."

"Not good." Her voice deepened with worry. "But we can't cancel on her. We pride ourselves on never doing that."

"Are you sure about this, Emma?" Steph grabbed her arm suddenly. "Oh, I just remembered something. She's a doctor."

"A doctor?"

"An OB/GYN."

Shock froze her in place. "How do you know?"

"I recognized the name on the schedule," she said, dropping her hand from her arm. "She's the new doctor that took over after my first OB/GYN left town a few years ago. She's really good."

Emma shook her head. Why hadn't Luke mentioned that last week? And, even more important, why would a woman intelligent enough to go through medical school marry an asshole like Mark Benjamin? What was wrong with her? He wasn't that great in bed, either. "I can't believe it."

"Well, it's a done deal." Her mother pressed her back and pushed her into the warm diner. "I'm cold and hungry."

Emma allowed her mother to drag her along. A rush of heat and laughter broke through the uncertainty of the situation. Her mother was right. It was a done-deal. Never before had Cooks decided against catering a wedding unless the customer was just too unreasonable and argumentative. And that rarely happened. Some bride's parents were more testy and obnoxious than others, but most could be reasoned with in the end.

Rebecca Greenlee. No, Dr. Rebecca Greenlee, didn't seem that way at all.

"Em?" Her sister tapped her back. "Why did you stop?"

She didn't say a word as her mother waved in her

general direction. Steph pushed at her back. "I see her, Steph."

Then she noticed someone else a few table behind her mother, sitting alone with a cup of coffee in front of him. "Shit."

"What?"

Emma tore her eyes from the now-staring man. "Nothing."

Keeping her head lowered as she wandered toward her mother was harder than it should have been. Awareness roared in her, heart beat hard under her breasts, lungs hurting for lack of oxygen. Never before had she reacted this way because of a man. She'd loved Frank with all her heart, and he'd never had her losing it. Her legs gave out when she reached the table, forcing her to grab for the back of her mother's chair. One stolen kiss a week ago shouldn't make her so feeble. Hormones, that all it was. Those stupid erupting hormones caused by the changes in her body because of her being pregnant.

Stupid damn sperm donor.

"You all right?"

No, she wasn't okay. "Just…hungry."

"Sit down, honey, before you fall down."

"I'm…fine."

"Yeah, right." Sarcasm dripped from both her sister's words. "You saw someone—" Eyes widening, she jerked her head beyond her table. "Someone you didn't want to see, I'm expecting. But who could it be?"

Before she could stop herself, she gazed at the still staring lawyer. A grin warmed his mouth now. "It's wrong. All wrong."

"Oh, wow," Steph whispered. "Who is that?"

Her mother twisted around. "Who are you two gawking at?"

"Mom," Emma said, heat flashing into her face. If she didn't take their focus of Luke, he would come over and talk. And that's the last thing she wanted. The first time they were alone she'd kissed him; the next time wouldn't end with a kiss. This damn hungry body of hers wouldn't allow him to leave until it was satisfied. *Hormones.* "Mom, Steph, stop it now. You're acting like idiots."

"Oops, he's coming." Steph laughed low. "Wow."
Dammit.

****

Luke had every intention of ignoring Emma and the two other women, yet his legs had a different idea. Before he could tell his mind how stupid going to her would be, he was standing and walking to the table.

"Emma?"

She didn't look up. "Luke."

The older woman smiled at him. "You know my daughter?"

"Yes," he said, stepping in closer to Emma's chair. Her shoulders stiffened at his approach. "We met last week."

"He's…the sperm donor's lawyer," Emma whispered. "Mark's brother."

"Oh?" The woman sighed loud at Emma's comment. "Don't let my daughter upset you, Mr. Benjamin. She's troubled about…things."

"I understand, Mrs. Cook." He relaxed a bit at her kind words and warm smile. An older version of her daughter's. "My brother can be hard to take at times."

And he did understand because he was as troubled.

42

He'd left her Friday night with every intention of never seeing her again. Yet he'd found his thoughts on her more and more as the week went by, on that kiss he'd forced on her. He still felt it heating his body and freeing his heart. That, more than any other thing, was the reason he'd stayed away. His reaction had scared him.

"Keep your head out of the gutter, Steph."

"I'm trying, big sister."

Emma snorted loud, sending the other woman bursting into laughter. "Stop it, Steph."

Only then did he realize what he'd said, and he shook his head. "I guess I should've worded that a bit differently."

"Yes," Emma's sister said, fighting down her laughter. "Oh, I'm Stephanie Williams, and this"—she pointed at the now observant older woman—"is our mother, Linda Cook."

"It's nice to meet you both." Luke nodded at the sister without taking his eyes off the older one "And your daughter didn't upset me, Mrs. Cook. My brother treated her with total disrespect. She has every right to feel the way she does."

A look of surprise widened in Emma's eyes.

"That's kind of you to say, Mr. Benjamin."

"It's the truth." Emma was clearly this woman's daughter. "Please call me Luke."

"All right, Luke, I'll do that. And you can call me Linda.

"Linda," he said.

"Mrs. Cook makes me sound too old." She pointed at the empty space at the table. "Would you like to join us?"

"No, he can't do that, Mom."

She ignored Emma's plea and waited for his answer. Even though he'd wanted Rebecca not to mention his new lady friend to his family, he still nodded and pulled a chair from the table behind him. He'd had time to think over his reason for wanting to keep Emma safe from them, and he realized it wasn't necessary. The agreement he'd made with the judge was between Mark and Emma, not him. And, for once, he would think about himself. Since meeting her last week, he'd been intrigued. Something about her had spoken to him then, and it only became louder and more real while they ate dinner and talked at her home. Something special had developed between them, something he wanted to mature to its fullest.

"Yes, join us," Steph said. "Emma didn't tell us much about what happened at the meeting between you and Uncle George."

"She didn't?" He placed the chair between Emma and her mother and settled into it. A waitress came by then. "Oh, I moved from the table over there. I hope that's okay."

"Yes, that's fine," she said, placing her pencil to the pad. "I saw you move. Would you like more coffee?"

"Yes, thank you."

She wrote it down and then grinned at Linda. "I can probably guess what the three of you want."

"Probably," the older woman said. "BLT and onion rings for me, hamburger with the works and fries for Steph, and a chicken salad sandwich for Emma."

"Done." The waitress didn't even bother writing on her pad. "And you all want unsweetened ice tea, right?"

"Yes," Emma said. "Can I add a side of cottage cheese with my sandwich?"

"Sure," she said, scribbling on the pad. She twisted his way. "I know you already ate, but maybe you'll like some pie or cake."

"Do you have apple pie?"

She nodded.

"I guess I'll have a slice of that." He leaned back into his seat. "Put it all on my bill."

"No." Emma sat up straight and firm beside him. "We can pay for our own food, Luke."

"Oh, be quiet, sis." Steph stretched out and pinched her cheek lightly. "Let your guy pay for our meal, why don't you?"

Your guy? Luke liked that. "Yes, let me pay."

He could tell she thought the whole thing was a bad idea, but he didn't care. Maybe if he hadn't followed her home and eaten her aunt's delicious lasagna, he might not be as willing to be seen with her. Maybe if she hadn't opened up a bit, talking so easily. Maybe if he hadn't kissed her.

"You're being unreasonable, Emma."

Linda leaned toward her quiet daughter. A part of Luke understood why she was acting this way, because of the agreement she signed with Mark. Yet another part knew the agreement had nothing to do with him. For the last two years, he'd been helping Mark out of one problem after another. Nothing as bad as getting another woman pregnant while engaged, but the complications were bad all the same. He was tired of putting his brother's wellbeing ahead of his own. He was tired of putting the family business and name ahead of his own needs. He loved his family, but...

He was weary of being alone.

"Oh, okay, he can pay."

"Good." Steph tapped her sister's clasped hands. "Now was that so *hard*."

Even he had to grin at the play on words. Too bad Emma wasn't in a playful mood now, because her response was only a loud outburst of breath. Luke pulled the chair closer to the table, making sure it was touching Emma's. Her body stiffened at his nearness, straightening against her seat. But instead of moving away, he placed his arm around her and caressed her taut shoulder.

"So everything is settled between my daughter and your brother?" Linda asked. "She didn't tell us much about what happened, and I haven't talked with George. Maybe you can't tell me everything, but surely you can tell a bit more than Emma has so far."

Luke glanced at the woman beside him. "Nothing that we discussed was for our ears only, Emma. It's okay to tell your mom and sister."

She shrugged. "I didn't feel like talking about it."

"Why?"

Emma placed her hands flat on the table and twisted toward him. His hand cupped her throat gently, enjoying the feel of her accelerated heartbeat against his skin. She softened under his touch and then jerked an inch away. "Why? You really want to know why?"

"Yes, I would." Irritation rose at her attitude. "Nothing bad was asked of you or my brother. Nothing out of the ordinary."

She groaned loud and then shook her head. "Oh, nothing unusual was suggested for either of us? Except for Uncle George setting up a trust fund for the baby and me having to prove that Mark is really the father, all was well. It didn't seem to matter if I wanted the money or not."

"The money is for the baby!" he exclaimed. "It's not for you."

"Like your family or Rebecca will believe that."

Luke froze at the mention of his old friend's name.

"Speaking of Rebecca," she said, leaning even further from him. "Why didn't you tell me she was a doctor? Here I always thought doctors were smart."

"She is," he said, taken aback by her attack change. "Rebecca graduated in the top twenty-five of her medical class."

"Oh, really?" She pointed her finger in his direction. "Then why is she marrying that asshole brother of yours? How come she doesn't see how bad he is for her? For any woman?"

"Honey, that's enough."

Luke didn't know what to say. The more he thought about it, the more he wondered. Hadn't Rebecca cancelled the engagement three times over the last two years? If she was truly sure of things, wouldn't she just marry him?

"He slept with me while engaged to her." She inhaled and exhaled hard on her words. "More than once."

"She broke off the engagement," he said, jumping to his brother's defense without thinking first. "He met you during that time. He wasn't thinking straight."

"Maybe one time," Linda said, forcing her way into their conversation. "Yet my daughter told me they dated for three months after that."

Damn, he didn't need this now. Thankfully, before

any more could be said, the waitress arrived with the food. Silence settled around the table as she placed the drinks in front of them, and then the meals. The last dish was filled with apple pie. He picked up his coffee cup and took a careful sip, glancing around the table at the eating women. Linda bit into her BLT while Steph smashed the top bun hard onto the bottom and picked it up. Emma sat frozen in her seat.

"You need to eat, Emma."

"I know that."

"Just eat slowly, honey," her mother said.

Emma gazed at her as if she didn't quite believe her before picking up one half of the sandwich and taking a small bite. She chewed and swallowed it down, waiting for a few seconds before taking another bite. She relaxed into her chair.

Even her eating was fascinating.

A half of her chicken salad was finished and most of the cottage cheese before he managed to pull his gaze away. Unfortunately, it landed on her grinning mother. This whole situation made him feel like a teenager on his first date with a girl. Yet he wasn't a kid, and this wasn't his first date. He was a grown man, a widower who only now found a possible path out of his grief. Emma had him feeling again, wanting to be with someone.

Linda set down her iced tea and laid her hand on his arm. "I like you."

"Mom?"

"Well, I do." A warm smile wrinkled around her mouth and eyes. "I only saw your brother once, on his way out of my daughter's home. He didn't impress me much."

Very intuitive woman. "Now I see where Emma gets her...outgoing attitude."

"I think George will be okay with the two of you dating," she said. "I am."

"Uncle George will be upset, Mom."

Emma leaned over slightly, causing his forgotten hand to slip along the soft skin of her neck. The tips of his fingers glided under the loose collar of her blouse. He swallowed and pinched the material around two fingers. She didn't pull away. Instead, she leaned in closer. Did she even notice her reaction? Luke didn't know, and he didn't care. All he knew was that he suddenly needed to feel her soft, naked skin. He needed to bath in the sweet, flowery scent issuing from her.

"Maybe, if things..."

He spread his fingers down the smoothness of her back and rubbed the tips over her tight neck muscles.

"This isn't...right."

"Feels right to me, Emma."

"Does it?"

Her look softened as she relaxed under his caressing finger. He sighed and spread his fingers wider, connecting to as much of her skin as possible. Like at the conference with her uncle and his brother, he lost his focus. All he sensed now was the warmth of her arm and the scent of spring flowers coming from her skin. All he remembered was that kiss. He hardened under her spell, forgetting that the two weren't alone at the table.

"I think it's time for us to leave, Mom."

The laughing comment barely registered in him.

"Yes, Steph, I do believe it is."

The soft hit against his back pulled him back to the

restaurant "You're leaving?"

Linda just nodded and followed her laughing younger daughter through the filled diner.

Emerald-colored eyes shined with sweet hunger.

Shit, but he wanted her. Right or wrong, he wanted her. "Are you ready to go?"

Emma sighed out a yes.

Chapter Five

Emma never made it back to Cooks to retrieve her vehicle. Luke insisted that he drive her home, and she was more than fine with it. He helped her into the car, slipping in quickly behind her. His arm fell across the back of the seat and settled over her shoulder. Like he'd done in the diner and like he'd done in front of Rebecca last week, he took away her choice.

Yet she didn't mind his high-handed attitude now.

Her body warmed at his closeness, heart beating fast and hard. A hot spicy scent settled around her, woodsy and warm. Stupid though it may be, she wanted to feel this man naked against her. She wanted to bury her head into that manly scent.

Luke turned off the freeway and onto her road, slowing into the parking space beyond her driveway. He stopped the vehicle and turned into her short drive.

"Are you changing your mind?"

He didn't look at her. "I should."

She laid her hand on his firm thigh, curving her fingers between his legs. "It's crazy, I know."

"Your lawyer won't be pleased, Emma."

Why did he have to bring that up? Mentioning her lawyer brought to mind the reason she needed one, and that made her remember that she wasn't actually free to get involved with a man. Especially this one.

"Forget I said that, babe."

"How can I forget, Luke?" Her caressing hand tightened on his leg, relishing the feel of its tautness. She needed to let him go, yet she couldn't. "You need to go—"

A loud growl echoed in the fancy car a second before his arm squeezed around her shoulder and the second hand cupped her face, lifting it up to his hungry lips. His kiss devoured her, stealing both her breath and her senses. She groaned out a frustrated sigh and clamped her fingers on his thigh as he buried his tongue in her mouth. She moaned again, slipping her clutched hand from his thigh to his chest upward to the side of his neck. His heart beat rough against her fingers as she moved them over his heated skin to the back of his head, and pressed her mouth up to match his desire.

Why deny her body the man? Why allow the past to interfere with the present? She wanted to be with this man because she wanted him, nothing else.

Right or wrong, she needed him.

"Inside," he growled out, releasing her mouth. He jerked his hand toward the door handle and pressed it open.

"Yes." He pulled her out of the car, walking beside her up the short steps. Her keys were in her hands and unlocking the door before she heard the unmistakable sound of a car locking in the quiet air. It opened with a bang a flash of a second later and he pushed her into the dim living room, slamming the door hard. Her coat fell to the floor followed by his, and then she kicked off her shoes. They landed near his discarded shirt.

"Luke?" She grinned at his eagerness, placing both of her hands on his hard chest and spread the fingers wide. "Nice."

This would be okay. She would be okay.

Her hands explored the width of his naked chest, down the hard abs to the button at the top of his jeans. He groaned when her hand rested on the bulge of his cock. Her legs weakened at the size of it, pussy going wet in anticipation of having him inside her.

"I never wanted...someone," she whispered, stroking his length through the blocking barrier of his pants. "Maybe it's because I'm—"

"Stop talking," he howled, lifting her and heading toward the back hallway. She let out her breath and allowed him to take control. "Bedroom?"

"Open door," she said, forcing in life-giving air. She sighed out the breath when he raced into the dark room and deposited her onto the bed, falling on top of her and covering her mouth once again with his. "Oh."

Urgency trembled in him, a need so strong she felt it in her own body. He deepened the kiss and then slipped his lips along her cheek to her ear, nibbling on it with devastating hunger before continuing his journey to her neck and shoulder. He slid out the top button of her blouse and then the second and third until he pulled the material completely apart. He jerked off the material and threw it to the floor. A second later her bra followed the blouse, and he laid her on the mattress. Warm breath moved over her breasts and then his tongue flicked the nipple, sending her upper body up and into him.

"Beautiful."

She wanted him. Now. "Luke?"

He lifted his mouth from her and looked into her eyes. "Don't say no, Emma."

All she could do was shake her head.

"It's not wrong," he whispered, placing both hands on the bed on either side of her head. "Feels…right."

"Yes." She moved her hands between their bodies, spreading them wide against his smooth, hard chest and traveling up to his shoulders. She grinned and pushed at his arm, toppling him to the side and twisting her body to land on top of him. He laughed at her maneuver before shaking his head and raising her easily off him to the floor. "Hey."

"Stay." He sat up and undid the button and zipper of her pants. They fell to the floor and she stepped out of them, leaving her in only small, light green panties. "That's a little better."

A delicious chill ran up her body. His hungry gaze overwhelmed her. That little voice deep inside tried to explain how wrong sleeping with him could be, but she silenced it. His seduction buried the memory of the last man she'd been with, as well as the reason for her out-of-character behavior that night. All she wanted to do now was enjoy this man, this one time. Then he would say goodbye and she would go on with her life. The way his brother had, the way her ex-husband had.

"Babe," he said softly, trailing his fingertips down through the valley of her breasts and her still-flat stomach. He spread his hands there, covering her in a net of safety. Then he stopped his movement, with concern peaking past his desire. "Is it safe? For sex?"

She nodded. Her OB/GYN had said it was fine to have sex. "It's safe."

"Good. "A growl roared from him. He moved his fingers down into her panties, sliding the tips of them over her middle. "Nice and wet."

And weak and ready, she pleaded whispered words

as he tore off her panties and placed her on her back. Then he kicked out of his shoes, grabbed a packet from his pocket, and stepped out of his jeans. Her heart warmed in a different way when he tore open the packet and slipped it on his cock.

"Luke, that's not…"

He groaned and attacked her breasts, flicking the edge of her nipples with a rough tongue. She swallowed the rest of her statement and moaned his name, pushing at the top of his head. He released the one he was working on and traveled his mouth and tongue over her stomach around to her outer thigh to her leg to her feet and back up the other side. She panted, aching with desire to feel his tongue on her aroused middle.

But instead of answering, he continued his journey back up her body until his mouth covered hers in a famished kiss. His hands held him a few inches off her, his hardness rubbing against her damp core. She opened her legs, delighting in the feel of him. He growled out his pleasure and eased slowly into her, a delicious, one glorious inch at a time until he was buried deep. He stopped then, lifting his mouth from hers.

"Don't stop, Luke."

He closed his eyes and pulled out of her, then thrust slow back inside. In and out, slow even strokes of pure pleasure, driving her just as slowly to the edge of fulfillment and then easing her back with the outward stroke. She moaned out his name and jerked her body, asking him without words to speed the process. He responded by thrusting hard and fast, lifting out quickly and thrusting again. With his quick, filling stroke her orgasm spread closer and closer to the surface, finally roaring out with his screamed name. She slammed up into him, taking all the pleasure he was willing to give her until he stiffened and thrust one last time. And fell on top of her, sweat mixing with her sweat, wood scent with her light floral perfume.

"Shit, babe."

All Emma could do was agree.

****

Luke lay on top of her for a few minutes, too weak to move. He finally found the strength to roll, pulling her with him so she lay soft at his side. One smooth, long leg over his firmer ones and one soft arm along his chest, he put his hand at the back of her head and placed her face into the dip of his shoulder. Sharp, quick breaths warmed the chilled skin there, racing heart beating hard and fast.

His brother had been right about her, yet Luke sensed there was more to this woman. She had taken a chance being with him tonight, and so had he. Even though her mother thought the judge would be pleased, Luke wasn't as sure. Maybe as her uncle, but definitely not as her lawyer. Luke's selfish need to make love to her may have left the deal in limbo. Technically, what she and her brother signed concerned only the two of them. Only the two of them needed to stay away from each other, not members of either family. Yet Rebecca found out about her, and he'd foolishly joined them at their table in a public place. He may not be as well-known as a Benjamin in the community as his parents or brother and younger sisters, but he was still known.

A calm touch settled against his chin, stopping his frantic thoughts. She buried her head in his neck and sighed. Damn, but he could get used to this woman. "That was nice."

"Just nice? A grin messed with her mock-serious voice. "You can do better than that, Luke."

"Probably." He traced his fingertips up her back and cupped her neck, kissing the top of her head. "Once my brain starts functioning again."

Sweet laughter warmed over his shoulder. "That'll work."

His gruff laughter mixed with hers. He loved the sound of her laughter, not to mention her voice. Calm and comforting, warm and sweet and full of life, it gave peace. Peace he hadn't realized he lacked. "I can listen to you laugh all day long."

"Good," she said, burrowing her head deeper into his shoulder. "Because you'll hear me laugh a lot."

"As long as you don't stop talking to me." He closed his eyes and relaxed into the bed. "That voice of yours really speaks to me."

Her laugh deepened at his unintentional wording.

"Let me rephrase that," he said, gathering her up tighter into his side. "What I meant to say is the sound of it, the warmth, surrounds me with peace. Like a serene waterfall or a crisp blowing wind."

Her laughter stopped and she gazed at him through half-closed lids. "Thank you, Luke. That was sweet." She hesitated for a second before adding, "Your brother never wanted me to talk at all. And my ex-husband—Frank and I seemed to talk everything out before we tried to have a baby. Then afterward—nothing."

He didn't want to respond, yet he sensed she needed him to react. "Sometimes people just…stop loving each other."

"Yes," she whispered, so low he barely heard. "Sad, but true."

Emma didn't say another word as the dim early evening light faded into darkness. Luke needed to leave now before someone recognized his car in her drive. Through his father's work with the town council and his mother's volunteering for every charity event held in the community, they knew many people. And with the planning of the annual Thanksgiving Festival—his mother's overall favorite charity—more individual town members than ever might notice his vehicle. His mother liked to borrow his BMW rather than use her own vehicle. He never could figure out why, however.

Chilly skin greeted his sliding touch as he rolled her onto her back, and she curled in a fetal position, sound asleep. Heat filled his heart at her innocent look. He slipped off the bed and placed the corner of the blanket over her, stepping away a bit. She snatched at his hand and turned on her back, a pleading request speaking loud in her wide eyes.

"I need to go, Emma."

Sadness lingered between them. "Just like Mark."

"No, I'm not like my brother."

"Leave then, if you want." She twisted away. "But you don't have to."

And he didn't want to go, yet. "Someone might see my car."

"I don't care," she whispered. "So what? We're not doing anything wrong."

Luke glanced down at the half-asleep woman. If it didn't bother her, why should it bother him? Did it really matter anyway? Rebecca knew about Emma, and no doubt she would mention it to Mark. No telling what his brother would do after finding out his Emma was the same woman he'd gotten pregnant.

"Stay, Luke."

Could something so right be wrong? Easy decision. "Lift up so I can pull the blanket all the way down," he said, yanking at the top of the heavy material. "You need to share it, you know."

Emma yelped and rolled away, laughter ringing out in the room again.

Monday would be soon enough to face Judge Brown and his brother.

This weekend he would enjoy her.

Chapter Six

Emma turned to her side and stretched out her arms. No one was in the bed. Her eyes filled with tears and she swiped them away. She shouldn't be upset. He wanted to leave last night, but she made him stay. At least he waited until she was fast asleep before he disappeared, unlike his asshole brother. It had barely been over when Mark got up to search for his clothes.

Something black caught her eye. She stepped from her bed, grabbed her robe and moved toward the object. One of Luke's shoes. Searching the room, she spied the second one half under the bed.

He hadn't left.

"I can't talk now."

The whispered words moved her to the kitchen, robe still in hand. She spied him at the sink, clad in his jeans with bare feet and a gloriously bare chest. What a pleasant thing to witness so early on a Sunday morning, a half-naked guy making coffee. The coffeemaker gurgled as the last of the water perked through, going silent a second later.

"I told you," he spoke into his cell, still not turning from the sink. "I'm not home, Mom."

Mom? He's talking to his mother, in her kitchen, while she was standing naked. She yanked on her robe and slashed it tight at her waist. What a silly way to react. His mother couldn't see her.

"Hey, babe."

"Good morning."

"I'm listening, Mom," he said, extending one arm. She settled against him. "I'm not alone."

She moved to his front, delighting in his uneasiness as well as his care. She winked and tapped his hip, placing both hands flat on his hard ass. He growled her name and pushed her away.

"No, I stubbed my toe." A frown took over his grin now. "What?" He listened to his mother for a long few seconds, and then said, "Rebecca shouldn't have said anything. She promised she wouldn't say anything until I—"

"Rebecca? She told your mother what she saw, didn't she? I didn't want anyone to know about us yet."

He placed his finger over his lips. "Yes, I'm with a woman."

Hesitation fumed into slight annoyance at his attitude. This would never have happened if he kept his hands to himself after their stupid meeting. A week ago. Had it only been a week? "It's your fault, Luke."

Luke shrugged and then said, "Yes, she a part of the catering place."

She shook her head hard at him.

"Her name is Emma."

She threw her arms up and raced out of the room. For someone who wanted to leave her last night because someone might recognize his car, to someone telling his mother everything about her the next day, didn't settle well with her.

Why didn't he leave like she half-expected him to do?

They'd had sex, just like she had sex with his

brother.

With his brother?

Damn, what had she done?

She sank onto her couch and buried her face in her hands. What must he be thinking? She'd given herself to him almost as easily as she gave herself to his brother. Yet the two weren't the same at all. His brother left without saying a word; he stayed. His brother didn't say much of anything to her, but Luke wanted to talk. Friday night they talked for hours without even realizing it. And he'd talked with her at the diner with her mother and sister, not to mention right now.

He wasn't the same type of guy.

"Emma?"

Overreaction maybe, yet she didn't want to see him now.

"I made coffee." A hint of laughter sang in his voice. "Want some?"

Tears threatened. *Stupid damn hormones.* "I can get it myself."

"No, I'll get it for you." Relief sounded in his tone. He set the phone on the stand by the door and raced back into the kitchen. A cabinet opened and closed, and then a second one opened before she heard him pull out the pot from the maker. It clinked back into place and he appeared at the door, two steaming cups in his hand.

"I make a mean cup of coffee," he said, teasing edge in his tone. "Good stuff."

She gripped the offered cup. Steam rose off it, the sharp scent of her favorite drink filled her nose. She loved the smell of coffee.

"Babe?"

"Don't call me that." She took a careful sip,

refusing to give in to his playful attitude. She wasn't sure why she was so upset. They had dinner together in public and his car had been sitting in her driveway all night. And this was a small town. "You told your mother my name. Why?"

"Rebecca already told her," he said, matter-of-factly. "Monday, she promised to keep what she saw a secret, yet…"

"Your mother used enhanced interrogation techniques on her." Sarcasm sang loud in her voice. "And she had to talk."

"Okay, I get it."

"You get what?" Staying mad at anyone was hard, yet it was impossible with a hot guy with bare feet and a smooth, touchable chest. Not to mention a sexy grin that set her heart racing. How can a woman stay upset at a man who'd had her screaming his name the night before? Who had her wanting to scream it again with just a silly grin? Especially when that woman wasn't sure why she was angry in the first place? "You did ask her not to tell anyone, so I guess that's something."

"Yes, I did ask her," he said, twisting to look at her. He brushed her hair out of her eyes. "Rebecca would have honored that promise, if she could. Mom must have heard something from someone else."

"Who?"

He shrugged. "I followed you home Friday night and joined you for dinner yesterday at the diner. Mom has a lot of friends."

"I was just thinking the same thing." Shouldn't Emma be more upset? And why did she suddenly want to touch him? "Pregnant lady hormones, I'm suspecting."

"You think so?" Luke fingered her hair and drew her close to his smirking mouth. "So does that mean you don't want me to leave?"

She curled her legs and turned toward him, placing her hand flat on his naked chest. He took in a hard breath when her finger dropped to his upper thigh. Shivers flowed across her skin, a sweet warm tingling sensation easing down her body. "What do you think?"

He growled her name in frustration and captured her mouth. She attacked his tongue with hers, smoothed it over the top of his mouth and pressed him back into the sofa. Her body erupted with need so hot and fast and hard it melted her core. It spread like the flame in a gas oven. She deepened the kiss, enjoying the control he gave her. Then she released his mouth, sat up, and untied the sash at her waist. The material fell open as she stood and let it drop to her feet. Her hands went to her breasts, cupping them hard. Luke jerked out of his pants and flung them to the coffee table. His cock stood proud and straight.

Moist longing raced through her body at the sight. But it was the yearning settling into her heart that froze her in place. How in the hell could love happen? In such a short time. With the brother of her sperm donor?

"Babe, I'm dying here."

Emma couldn't move. No, she couldn't be falling in love with this man. It was sex, that's all. Only sex. This whole thing had to be because she was pregnant. Wanting him so desperately right now, after being upset at him, didn't make any sense if her hormones weren't so out of control.

"Babe, come here."

He rose easy from the sofa and took her hand,

pulling her on top of him. Penis resting hard and ready between her thighs, lips tracing a line of heat and need over her forehead and nose to her chin before angling over her mouth once again. He lifted her, positioning her over his arousal and slowly joined their bodies. She came to life then and took over the movement, raising her upper body from his and lifting off him. One foot on the floor and one hand clasping the back of the sofa, she rode him until a fierce orgasm slammed into her. She shook with the sweet brutality of it, thrusting again and again until he stiffened and growled her name. He grabbed her hips and jerked up a few times before pulling her into a weak kiss.

Then the only movement was his chest rising fast to meet her sensitive breasts. The only sounds were the rasping of their breaths.

"I could get used to this," he whispered a few second later, breath warm against her slightly bruised mouth. "My brother said you were—"

His groan blocked out the rest of his words. Emma didn't care to hear them. Nothing that his asshole of a brother said interested her. Neither did what he thought or wanted. Or, she suddenly realized, she didn't care what Uncle George thought, or the Benjamin clan, or anyone else. All she cared about was what Luke thought.

"Mom wants to meet you." His whisper echoed loud in the quiet room. "I told her someday, but not yet."

Emma let out a sigh and then lifted her head from his shoulder. "I'd like to meet her, Luke."

His eyes widened in surprise. "Really? You would?"

"Yes," she said, resting her head back into his shoulder. "Mark was a mistake, you're not."

He went quiet at her statement. Except for loud inhales and the rapid beat of his heart against her cheek, he didn't move or react. Then he exhaled one long, deep breath warm over her hair, lifting it gently from her head, and encircled his arms soft around her waist.

She could get used to this.

"She mentioned something about the Thanksgiving Festival, the early Thanksgiving dinner on Sunday," he said, tender excitement in his voice now. "It's two weeks away."

"Cooks is one of the places catering that dinner," she said.

"Benjamin Winery has a booth at the festival this year," he said. "I'm going to be helping Mom on Friday and Saturday. We got a table set up inside the community hall to sell our wine for the Christmas charity."

The holiday season would be the perfect time to meet his parents, if it was okay with her family. Thanksgiving would be the first holiday her mother celebrated without her father. So shouldn't she be spending the day with her?

"You don't need to decide now, babe."

"No, I want to meet her. I'm helping Mom, Steph, and the aunts with the dinner, so I'll already be there." She rose from him and settled into the opposite corner of the couch. He raised his bare feet into her lap, stretching his body out the length of the sofa. She skimmed her fingernails down the rough bottom. "Cute."

Luke placed his hands under his head and winked.

"So are you."

She just shook her head. "How can two brothers be so different?"

He brushed his foot into her arm. "Does that mean you like me?"

"Well, let's put it this way," she said, tickling the bottom of his foot again. "You are more charming than your brother."

"That's a good thing." He snorted to keep from laughing. "Seeing that you think Mark's an asshole…"

"He is," she said, with less anger and heat as usual. "But I'm not exactly innocent."

"No, not even close."

The words were harsh yet his smirk told her he was joking. She relaxed into the sofa and crossed her arms over her breasts. His eyes narrowed and then he stood and reached for his pants and her robe. He threw her covering at her, and slipped into his jeans. Disappointment filled her when he sat at the far end of the couch, completely clothed.

"I can tell you need to talk, babe." He pushed the robe closer. "If you want my full attention, you need to cover that delicious body of yours."

Emma pushed away the sudden tears and tied her robe tight around her. She wasn't sure if the tears were because of his sensing she wanted to talk or that he was willing to listen. Or maybe it was just more of those hormonal outburst caused by the little one growing inside her.

"You okay?"

She straightened up so quickly she pressed into the cushion. "Yes, I'm fine." Concern still lined his eyes. "Why?"

He touched the hand she'd spread wide on her stomach, caressing his fingers over it. "I thought something was wrong with…the baby."

Oh, damn, why did he have to be so kind? Why did he have to show he cared? Tears wet her cheek.

"Emma?"

She took in one mouthful of air after another until her emotions settled down. "Stupid hormones."

His concern changed to bewilderment. "Hormones?"

Would she ever get control of her feelings during this pregnancy? She didn't remember her sister crying at every single kind word or act of caring.

"Emma?"

She waved him away again, and took in another breath. What the hell were they talking about?

"You want to talk, Emma?"

This time she controlled her reaction. Without thinking over what would come out, she said. "Do you know why I slept with your brother that night?"

"You were drunk," he said, hint of laughter in his tone. "You were horny.'

"Yes," she said. "I was drunk."

"But you weren't horny?"

A slow amount of joy from earlier rose in her. "Not as much as I was with you."

"Was?"

"Am," she said. "With you."

"So you slept with me because you needed to scream my name?"

His teasing question wasn't far from the truth. "Yes."

"Good." Satisfaction and pride revealed clear in his

demeanor. "I can live with that reasoning for now."

Good thing because that's the only explanation she was giving. The rest of her motivation was too new. If this was only about sex with Luke, it would be fine. Without love, even the best sex gets boring. That's why his brother not showing up one day didn't bother her that much. But with Luke, it'd be different. She already sensed it.

He pushed her leg with his bare foot, bringing her out of her thoughts. This man made her feel safe and secure in both body and spirit. "Mark was in the right place at the right time. Or maybe it was the wrong time."

"Yes," he said, dropping his foot on the floor. He picked up his forgotten, empty coffee cup. "I'll get us refills."

She wrapped her arms around her curled legs. "Thank you."

Emma closed her eyes as he moved around in the kitchen. Soon he appeared in the living room with two cups. He handed one to her and settled into the corner of the couch, giving her space.

"You're nothing like Mark," she whispered again. "He never did anything nice for me."

He stayed quiet and sipped his coffee. "So why did you get with him? What caused it?"

"It's a long story." Emma had a feeling he knew a bit about her past, her marriage. Uncle George said he would check out her and the business. Her divorce was common knowledge, but not the reason for it. Unless his investigator talked with mother or sister—or Frank himself—he wouldn't know anything about her two years of trying to get pregnant. "Well, I can make it shorter. For years Frank and I tried to have a baby, and we couldn't. He blamed me for it. That's what led to our divorce."

"You ex-husband blamed you?"

She shook her head, looking down at her coffee. "According to the doctor who checked us both out, he didn't have any problems."

"And you did?"

"No, I didn't either," she whispered. "The day I met your brother at that bar I saw Frank and his new wife. And she was very, very pregnant."

"Oh?"

"Yes, oh. That just kind of confirmed that it was my fault." Her grasped tightened around the hot cup. "That's where I was when I went into that bar with some old college friends. I didn't even worry about a possible pregnancy." Anger washed like fire through her. "It wasn't until three weeks ago when I missed a period that I suspected I might have been wrong." She swallowed her temper. "I got a home pregnancy test and it came back positive. I redid the test, and it still turned blue."

"That's when you realized you didn't even know his last name?"

Shame rose in her. "Mark's not the only bad person here. I am too."

"No, you're not."

Emma wanted to believe him, but what else would you call it. What else would you call a woman who picks up a man in a bar and has sex with him more than a dozen times, and still doesn't get his last name? The fault is as much hers as it was Mark's. "I saw a picture of him and Rebecca in the newspaper, announcing their engagement. I felt like such a fool."

"Don't even think that, Emma." His foot tapped her lower leg gently. "No one's perfect, you know. We all make mistakes."

She looked over the raised cup to his face. His expression looked far away, as if seeing one of his own clear in his mind. She leaned forward quickly, spilling a few drops of the liquid onto her bare knees. "I hope that look isn't because of me."

Luke shook his head. "Never you, babe."

"Good." Relief calmed her shoulders into the cushion. She wiped the liquid from her legs and sipped. "So what took you away?"

"You noticed that, did you?" His tone lightened a bit. "Only one other woman ever knew me that well."

"Kathleen?"

"Yes, my wife." He pulled his leg away and sat straight on the couch, glancing into the kitchen. "Kathleen was one of Rebecca's friends from college." His head lowered at the memories. "It just took one look and I knew she was the one for me. We married less than a year later."

"It took Frank and me three years," she said, grinning at the sweeter reminders of her past. "We dated seven or eight months before we even kissed."

"Didn't take me that long to kiss Kathleen," he whispered. "Yet, if you want to know the truth, it took a little longer than it took me to kiss you."

"You were grieving," she said. "For two years."

"Did I tell you that?" He studied her for a moment before shrugging. "But you're right. I was still grieving for her." He stopped speaking as he drank his coffee. "I think we need to get something to eat."

"Yes." She leaped from the couch. Thankfully no coffee spilled this time.. She waved toward him. "You stay here and I'll make us breakfast, Luke."

Instead of obeying, he stood and pointed toward the kitchen door. "After you."

Chapter Seven

Luke followed Emma into the kitchen. Why had he mentioned Kathleen? When his wife died in that car accident, he'd believed he would never find another woman to take her place. He expected to be alone. Until a week ago when he looked up into this woman's eyes and saw her pain. She'd been grieving also, in her own way. More for a marriage that had gone wrong than for a mistake with the wrong man, he realized.

"Sit down," she said. "I'll heat you something." She opened the refrigerator and searched through the covered dishes. "I think I have some breakfast burritos in here." She leaned over and partially pulled out one of the containers. "Yes, here it is."

Damn, but he could watch this woman all day. "From one of your aunts?"

"No." She lifted the dish and placed it on top of the stove, taking a couple of plates from the nearby cabinet. She grinned over her shoulder. "This is from my mom."

"Oh?" His heart warmed. It'd been doing that a lot the past two weeks. Even with Kathleen it hadn't happened this quickly, with totally unexpected, unwanted results. Until the stuff between her and his brother was finalized, he needed to keep his heart out of things. If it wasn't already too late. "My mother has a cook and maid."

"Your mother is part of one of the richest family in

the area," she said, softness lessening her sharp remark. "Oh, sorry, that was unfair."

"Truth is never unfair, Emma."

She didn't say anything as she placed two burritos on one of the plates, opened the microwave and set it on the glass. The machine buzzed. She twisted to face him. "So tell me about Kathleen."

If he thought she was going to forget about it, her question tore that hope away. And he wanted to tell her. He wanted her to know everything. "She was Rebecca's friend…"

"From college," she finished his thought.

"Yes." Taking his cup, he sipped the rich, hot liquid. "Small, blonde and beautiful, just like Rebecca, yet she was so different. Quieter, shyer, a bit unsure." He grinned over the rim. "I lost my heart almost at first sight."

"That fast?" She poured herself a cup of coffee and moved to the table, a smirk lining her sweet mouth. "It didn't happen that fast for me. Well, not until—" She stopped her words. The microwave dinged and she raced to it, pulling out the heated plate and putting in the second one. She snatched two forks from a small drawer and handed him the plate, setting both forks on the table. "You married eight months later."

A part of him wanted to find out why she'd stopped speaking, nevertheless he let it go. "Yes, I just started working for Benjamin Industries as a lawyer consultant. Fresh out of law school when we married. She was a nurse, worked at a hospital in Columbus." When Emma didn't say a word, he continued, "She commuted to work every day. We lived near my parents. She was fine with the drive, but I was a nervous about it. Especially in the winter time."

"Yes, winter driving is bad in Ohio," Emma said. "A year before my divorce I started working with my parents. I had to drive from Columbus to Bridgeview. Some days were worse than others."

"That day Kathleen died," he said, reliving the cop standing at the door, hearing him tell the bad news. "We had a fight before she left for work. She wanted to start a family, but I…" He shook away the memory. "Snow was falling hard. Kathleen was a good driver, careful, yet she was upset. She was crying when she left the house."

Emma grasped his hand. "You feel like it's your fault?"

"Yes, then I did." He turned his hand to tangle their fingers together. "I soon realized I wasn't at fault. Sure, we had an argument. But we'd had arguments before and she drove to work safely. In both good and bad weather." He tightened her fingers, enjoying the warm, non-judgmental contact. "My in-laws still haven't forgiven me."

She nodded, but didn't comment. The buzzer dinged a second time, sending her flying from the counter. He put down his cup and grabbed one of the forks. She settled back into her seat and snatched the second fork.

"I understood why they acted that way," he said, cutting into his burrito. He slipped the fork into the piece but didn't pick it up. "Kathleen was their only child." He bit into the food and chewed it, grinning at the burst of flavor. "Wow."

She grinned. "I bet my mom's cooking is better than your mom's cooking." Her eyes widened in a mocking way. "Oh, I forgot. Your mother's like me. She can't cook."

Peace filled him at her teasing words. "I never said she couldn't cook, I said she never had to."

"Oh, excuse me."

Her laughter rang out, erasing the lingering pain caused by his in-law's lack of forgiveness. He picked up a piece of the burrito shell and threw it at her.

"Hey," she said, smiling wider. "Stop wasting my food."

His heart did a little flip inside his chest. Falling in love with Emma was all wrong.

Too bad his heart wasn't listening.

****

Emma talked and teased with the man the rest of that day, stopping only long enough to tear his clothes off and make love to him. That night they fell into bed naked, and stayed that way until the sun rose Monday morning. A different ache assaulted her when she woke to find him searching the room for his clothing. The situation held at bay now battered her senses. No matter how it hurt she couldn't see Luke again, not until Mark told his parents and Rebecca about her. Not until he made things right.

Sadness filled her as Luke dressed, hurting more than she thought she would. In a short time, this sexy, hot, caring man had touched her. Not just her body but her heart. Seeing him leave wasn't easy, knowing she may never be with him again.

"Asshole," she whispered.

Luke stopped his movement. "Oh, I'm sorry. I didn't mean to wake you up."

"You were just going to leave?" Downheartedness

rather than anger spoke the question. "Is that it?"

He shook his head. "I was going to write you a note."

"A note?"

"What's wrong?" When she didn't answer quick enough, he stepped to the bed and sat. His fingers combed her mussy hair from her face, tracing light against her cheeks. "You think I want to leave?"

No, but it was necessary. Just like it was important she let him do it without a scene. "You don't have any choice, Luke."

"Because I have to go to work," he said, refusing to see the truth. "But tonight, I'll be back."

"No." She glanced down before she saw his reaction. "You can't come back. We can't see each other again. It's too...dangerous." He still didn't say anything, or move from his frozen position. "The last few days we forgot why it isn't possible for us."

"It's not impossible, babe."

He spoke the right words, yet his tone said he didn't believe them. She placed her hand over his. "Did you forget I'm carrying your brother's baby? And that I'm not supposed to have anything to do with him, or his family?"

"No, just with him."

"Luke, I can't do this." Tears ran down her cheeks. This time she let them flow. "It doesn't matter if I want to be with you or not, I can't. What will happen when your parents find out about me and Mark? When Rebecca does?" She focused on his blank face, trying to see something in it. Yet she couldn't. Like the first time she'd ever seen him, no emotion showed in his eyes. "You know it's the right thing to do, Luke."

"Why?" Anger flushed his face so suddenly she jerked her hand from his. "I don't agree with your conclusion, Emma. Just because things will be uncomfortable doesn't mean we have to stop seeing each other."

"What?" Slamming his hand away, she jumped from the bed and placed her hands hard on her naked waist. Naked and unafraid, too pissed off to see that he had the advantage, she stood straight and tall. "So being uncomfortable isn't important?" She crossed her arms around her middle, backing away from him. The nightstand blocked her motion. Yet it didn't matter. Luke had slipped off the bed and moved toward the bedroom door. "So you're really leaving?"

His shoulder sagged under his tight T-shirt. "You want me to go."

"No, I don't want you to go," she said, pleading now for him to understand. "I want you to stay, but you can't."

"Why?" He turned his head then. "Why can't I? If I want to stay with you, why can't I?"

Why was he being so dense? Why didn't he see the reason he had to leave now?

"You think your opinion is the only one that matters." Fierce hopelessness and anger burned in his eyes. "But it isn't, Emma. I have a say in this relationship. And I don't want it to end."

Neither did she, but...

"I'm not allowing Mark or my family to win," he said, hard, sad eyes pierced into her. "I'm not allowing the judge to dictate whom I can love." He jerked his hand forward and grasped at the doorknob, throwing it open and racing into the hall. He froze in place halfway to the living room before he turned. "Or you."

His last words rang out long after the front door closed behind his racing footsteps, cutting her deep with the truth. Did he even realize what he said? Did he hear his own words, or was he deaf to them? Did he really mean them?

I'm not allowing the judge to dictate whom I can love.

How could she allow this to happen? How could she have fallen in love with Luke so easily, so quickly?

Or you.

And, more importantly, how could she stay away from him? How could she stay away from someone who made her feel so alive and free? So hopeful and cared for? So loved?

"Mark has to tell Rebecca," she whispered. "Luke has to make him do the right thing for once."

A hint of hope leaped in her. She walked into the living room and found her cell phone, searching through the numbers and pressing Send. The phone rang once, twice, three times before a voice answered. "Mark, this is Emma."

"Why are you calling me?" Dismissal sang in his bitter words. "I have nothing to say to you."

"Don't worry," she said, feeling a rush of anger at his attitude. "I won't take up much of your precious time." He breathed loud as if in relief. She grinned. "I just called to give you one chance to make things right."

"What? Are you threatening me?"

"No." Did a lie to an asshole like him mean anything? "I'll tear up the agreements we signed last week, if you tell Rebecca about me."

"I can't do that." Anxiety raised his voice an octave. "I'm okay with the agreement."

Emma let go of her held breath—and her anger. "Is that your final answer?"

"Yes."

"Fine," she said, letting her temper free completely. "If you won't do the right thing, I'll have to do it for you."

"What?"

"Your choice, Mark."

Before he could respond, she slammed the End button and threw the phone to the sofa. It slid off the cushion and landed hard on the floor.

Chapter Eight

Luke shouldn't have come in to work today. He should've stayed with Emma and convinced her they deserved a chance. Instead he just sat at his desk, accomplishing nothing productive. Thankfully no work was due anytime soon. He had to return a few calls, and needed to finish an offer for another restaurant in Cincinnati Dad was interested in, yet Dan hadn't researched the place fully yet. He had time before he needed to talk to the board about that acquisition. The phone calls could wait a few days.

Thank God, because he was worthless today.

And it was all Emma's fault. Like one night would be enough for him. Like he was his brother, and he wouldn't want to see her again.

Why did she think she had the right to decide for both of them anyway? Why did she think he wouldn't want to talk about the situation she was in with his brother? Between them they could have found a solution, one where they could be together.

"Damn her."

He slammed his hand into the desk before jerking from his seat and racing to the window. Cars lined the parking lot this early in the morning, light rain falling around them. He glanced at his dark BMW. His brother's older model SUV slipped into the space beside it. The engine ran in the cold, damp air for a few minutes, then he slammed the door open and hurtled out of it, shutting the door with a livid blast of energy. The sound echoed all the way to Luke's third floor office. Hopefully Mark wouldn't show up at his door. The last thing Luke wanted to do now was take care of another one of his brother's problems.

Unless... He stood straight. "Has Rebecca found out about Emma?"

A ringing interrupted his wish-filled thought and he stepped slowly toward his desk. He picked up the phone and said his standard greeting. When the man greeted him back, he wished he'd stayed at the window. "Good to hear from you, Judge Brown."

"You might not think that way after we talk," he said, in a non-threatening way. "I talked to my sister Sunday, Emma's mother."

"Everything is fine, Judge."

Judge Brown muttered something Luke couldn't understand. He wasn't sure he wanted to know anyway.

"Bet you didn't know," the judge said, in a controlled way, "that both her mother and sister went to her house at different times, on Sunday. Both times your car was sitting in her driveway."

"Shit."

"Yes," he said, tone a bit more normal. "Personally, I'm glad she found a new man. Yet why does it have to be you? You know better, Luke. This could be very bad for Emma and her unborn child."

"I know," he said, standing and moving toward the window. His brother was nowhere in sight. "I wasn't thinking."

The man actually laughed at his comment. "You Benjamin men are fast workers."

He groaned. "I'm usually the careful, logical one. But with Emma…"

"She's special," he said, squealing his chair as he moved in it. "Frank didn't deserve her. He really hurt her with his accusation." He stopped talking, and then asked, "Did she tell you about her marriage and divorce? The reason for it?"

"About them trying to have a baby, yes," he said, fighting the unbelieving indignation the memory caused him. "That he made her believe it was her fault. When she saw him with his new, pregnant wife, she believed it too."

"You two talked?"

The disbelief in his voice eased his anxiety a bit. "Well, we talked too."

"Good." The old man laughed again. "You left her happy this morning?"

He wished he could lie and say yes, yet he couldn't lie to this man. Somehow he would know it wasn't the truth. "No, I didn't."

"Then that explains Mark's frantic voice message to me around seven."

He pulled the phone from his ear. Putting the phone back to his ear, he said, "Mark called you. Why would he do that? He's supposed to talk to me and then I relay the message to you."

"He did call you, Luke," the judge said. "He said he called your home and then your cell, but you didn't answer. Then he called me."

"I went home, but only long enough to get a shower, shave, and brush my teeth," he said, stepping to his chair again but not sitting down. "And I left my cell phone at Emma's."

"Oh, that explains it," the judge said.

Luke settled in his chair and pulled it tight to the desk. "So what did he say?"

"Not much. What he did say didn't make much sense to me."

"Tell me what he said."

"Let me check my cell," he said, turning on the speaker. "Can you still hear me?"

The judge's voice came in muddled, but Luke could hear him well enough. "Yes."

"Good."

A light beeping sound crackled from the speaker. "Hold on now, son."

"I'm holding."

A second later the phone went off speaker and he said, "I was going to let you hear it, but it'll be easier for me to just repeat it." He stopped speaking for a minute, then he said, "First he says my name, and he says that you aren't answering your phone or cell." He listened to the rest of the message. "Here's the good part. 'She threatened to tell Rebecca if I didn't.' "

"Who?"

"He didn't say," he said quickly, still listening to the message. "He also mentioned something about an agreement. That the woman calling would tear it up if he did the right thing."

"Emma?"

"That's what I was thinking, son."

Shit, what has she done? "She disregarded the agreement, not my brother."

The judge only let out a loud breath.

"I just saw him arrive to work. I'll talk to him." He rose from his seat once again and wandered into the outer office. Dan, his legal assistant, glanced up at him, a questioning look in his eyes. He waved and pointed at the phone. "I'm on my way to his office now."

Dan's eyes narrowed.

"I'll let you know what happens," he said. "Give me an hour or so."

"Good," the judge said. "I'll talk to Emma. Talk to you soon."

"Fine." He ended the call and told Dan. "I'm going to my brother's office."

"Do you need any help?"

"No," he said, forcing in calmness he didn't feel. "It's personal."

He nodded. "You're expecting a few calls. Should I forward them to Mark's number?"

"No." He handed Dan his phone. "Could you replace this for me?"

Dan nodded. "Sure."

"I'll be back in an hour or so." He moved through the door before his assistant could respond, toward the line of elevators at the other end of the hallway. "We're going to settle this once and for all, big brother."

****

"Mom, I think we should make pizza rolls and fruit skewers for the kids," Steph said, sitting in the stool beside Emma. "We need to make something healthy for the kids too. They'll have all those apples they pick in the orchard, but most parents won't allow them to eat them."

"You're right, Steph." Her mother moved from the main stove to the sink. "People are planning on making pies and other things with them." She dried her hands and moved toward Emma and her sister, settling on the remaining stool. "I just hope the weather gets better. Otherwise, it's going to be a bad time to pick those apples on Saturday."

Emma should make an attempt at speaking, if only her mind would focus on the conversation longer than a second or two. All she could hear was that phone call to Mark. Why had she done it anyway? No doubt she'd messed up everything. She may not have been happy about the stipulations placed on her, but that trust fund would go a long way paying for the child's college. The more she thought about it, the more she liked the thought of Mark paying out that six figure amount.

"Not to mention, taking the open wagon tour to check out the changing leaves," Steph added, frowning in her direction. "Or the display and food booths for the charity drive half the council members still insist should be set up along Main Street."

"All of them will be inside the conference hall this year," her mother said. "That was voted on by the committee last night. They'll be set along the front and side walls, leaving the back wall for the catering base and the dessert tables. The center of the room will have the decorated tables same as last year. It might be a bit crowded but at least everything will stay dry."

"I would have voted the same way if my youngest hadn't gotten sick," Steph said. "That's the important thing."

"You did," their mother added. "I voted for both of us."

"Good." She grinned and then faced her. "What do you think, Emma?"

"What?" Emma forced her mind off the call to Mark for the twentieth or so time since coming into the kitchen. "I'm sorry. I can't seem to concentrate."

"You've been this way all day, Emma," she said, bafflement rising slightly in her sister's voice. "What's bothering you anyway?"

"I said I was sorry," she said, again. "You were talking about the finger foods you two are planning on making for the kids."

"Yes, five minutes ago." Steph leaped from her stool and leaned close. "Maybe you should tell us what you did."

Guilt roared through her. She swallowed it down and tore her look from her concerned sister to her quiet mom. "If you didn't leave the diner Saturday night, it wouldn't have happened."

"Don't blame Mom and me." Steph placed her hands on her hips. "And I doubt your sleeping with Luke has you all twisted up inside, worried about something bad happening. That's not you at all."

"Your sister is right, honey."

No, what others thought of her never bothered her much. Some people had to talk about others. Emma was watchful in her personal life, however. Cautious and wary on whom she brought into her business decisions and her sex life. Mark had been a mistake, yes, but Luke was right. The more she thought on it, the more she sensed this truth.

And that was why she'd been so out-of-it today. The way she'd left things this morning with him didn't feel right. His face had been so emotionless when he'd walked out the front door. It hurt remembering.

Then she had to go and call Mark.

That was a thorough blunder.

"There she goes again." Her sister's teasing voice

pulled her off the phone call.. "I'm not letting this go until you tell us what you did." She waved a hand at her. "We know you had sex with Luke, so that's not it. What else happened this weekend?"

A single tear flowed, running unchecked down her cheek to her chin. She wiped it away, but another one took its place. Soon wetness flooded out as the last few days rose up to hurt her.

"Oh, shit, Em." All teasing faded from her sister's voice. "I didn't mean to make you cry."

"You didn't," she whispered. "I chased him away. I told Luke I didn't want to see him any more."

"You what?" Her mother stood from her stool and wrapped her arms around her. "Why would you do that, honey?"

"I had to," she said, choking out the words. "The agreement I signed with Mark says I can't be near him or him me. We can't have any contact with each other."

"I don't understand," her mother said. "You didn't have any contact with the baby's father. You've been with Luke."

"Luke is his brother." She settled her face against her mother's neck. "His mother knows Luke was with someone this weekend, someone named Emma."

"How?"

"She called his cell." Emma forced down another wave of tears and focused on the overlaying guilt. Her mother released her then. "He was in the kitchen, making coffee, talking to his mother. I said something and she heard my voice."

"So?" Steph sat back in her seat. "He's a hot, good-looking, rich, available male. I'm sure his mother isn't surprised he was spending the night with a woman."

"That's not it."

"And most of the Benjamins don't know you're carrying Mark's child," Steph said, lightly. "Except for your guy and his father. Mrs. Benjamin will just see you as her son's new lady, that's all."

"That's not all." Emma couldn't believe these two women. Couldn't they see how bad this was? How she'd messed up everything because she couldn't keep her hands off Luke. And then she doubled up by calling Mark. "You don't understand."

Neither her sister nor mother said a word until the silence turned uncomfortable. Then her mother settled back onto her stool, and whispered, "If only the baby's father was a better man. He would tell his fiancée the truth. Everything would be out in the open then."

"Yes, but he won't do that."

The dinging of the shop front door bell rang at the same time Emma's phone sang out an old tune. "It's Uncle George." She accepted the call. "Hi, Uncle George."

"Hey, sweetheart, we need to talk." The voice came from both the phone and the entrance doorway. She ended the call and faced the frowning man. "You found out about the call, didn't you?"

All he did was nod as he wandered through the kitchen to the back area. He pulled out a stool from the wall and sat. "What were you thinking?"

"I wish I could tell you." Rather than thinking, Emma had been reacting to the way Luke left. "I made a mistake."

"Yes, you did." Her uncle said. "But it can be fixed."

"What call?" Her sister and mother asked at the

same time. Then her sister added, "Is this the reason you've been so out of it today?"

"Yes," she said, wiping at her wet cheeks. "I called Mark and gave him a choice, either he tells Rebecca, or I do. If he told her about me and the baby, I would tear up the trust fund and medical records agreement."

"Honey, what were you thinking?"

The judge laughed, lightening the atmosphere in the room. "Surely you haven't forgotten what it was like to be young, little sister."

"No, I haven't forgotten," her mother said, warm remembrance laughing in her voice. "But Emma is over thirty. She's not young any more."

"Well, compared to you and me," George said, lightly. "She is."

Her mother stared at her brother for a long, quiet second before nodding. "Well, I'll give you that."

"And it may not be that bad."

Was her uncle's age getting to him? How could her action not be bad? She messed up big-time. For the hundredth time since seeing that positive result on the first stick, she wished she'd never gone out to dinner with her friend that night. If she'd stayed home with a bottle of wine, she wouldn't have seen her ex-husband's pregnant wife.

"So what can we do to minimize the problem?" Hope sprang soft in her mother's voice.

"There's nothing, Mom." Emma stood from the stool and stepped to the nearest sink. Maybe Mark was right. Maybe taking care of the problem was the only way out of their dilemma. "If there is no baby, then—"

A resounding *No!* rang out from the three in the room. Steph added, "Killing the baby isn't a solution,

Emma."

"You're not thinking straight again, honey." Her mother spoke at the same time, disbelief and anxiety deepening her voice. "You're talking about my first granddaughter here."

"You don't know it's a girl," Emma said, a new type of pain radiating down her body. "And I wouldn't do anything so...wrong anyway. I could never murder my child, just to make the sperm donor's life easier."

"No one believed you would, Emma. We know it's just frustration making you say things like that." Her uncle waved his hand toward her empty stool. She sighed and settled on the seat, wrapping her arms around her middle. "You and Luke were together, right?"

Shock roared in her. "How did you know that?"

"He told me," her uncle said with a patient smile. "Mark called a little after seven and left a message, and I called Luke around eight."

"Mark called you?"

"When he couldn't get his brother, he left a frantic message, something about a woman threatening to tell his fiancée about his indiscretion."

"Maybe someone should," her sister said, fury in her voice. "Mom and I met that doctor a few days ago. She's a nice lady, deserves better than someone like Mark."

Yes, Emma remembered the few hours Rebecca was with them. She'd hidden in her office like a coward until she left the building. Even after Steph called and told her the doctor wanted to talk with Luke's new lady, she refused to leave the room. She'd never acted that unprofessional before, and she didn't plan on doing it again. Hiding wasn't the answer any more than having an abortion would be.

"Luke promised to talk to his brother," her uncle said. "He'll call me back when he's done. If anyone can get that man to do the right thing, it'll be Luke. I think the elder Mr. Benjamin may get involved too."

A secretive, knowing look passed from her uncle to her mother, and then they both grinned. "What have you done, Uncle George?"

"Nothing bad. Let's just say I…introduced myself to the elder Benjamin."

Emma jumped from her seat.

"Sit down, niece." Her uncle patted the stool. "Mr. Benjamin won't get involved unless Luke can't talk his brother into doing the right thing."

"It won't make any difference. I'm sure the elder Benjamin will protect Mark like Luke does," Emma said, letting go of the tentative hope. "Rebecca may be his oldest friend, yet he'll still respect his brother's selfish action and do nothing to protect her."

"We'll see, honey." Her mother slid from her seat and beckoned to Steph. "Now I think it's time we make our final decision on what snacks to make for everyone at the festival."

Uncle George grinned. "Can I help test them?"

"And me," Emma added. "I know I have stuff to take care of but I don't think I can manage it now."

"Sure, honey."

"As long as you don't think you're going to help cook anything," her sister added, with a loud snort. "We just got the place aired out from your last attempt."

Emma would put up with her sister's mocking if it kept her from thinking about her problems.

Chapter Nine

"So you're telling me you won't do the right thing?" Luke stood tall in front of his brother's desk clutching his hands into fists. "Like Rebecca doesn't deserve the truth?"

Mark jerked from his seat and walked around the desk. He stopped in front of him, anger matching anger. "What is it with you? That agreement you made me sign last week made it all go away."

"You think so?" Luke straightened to his full height, four inches over his brother, and leaned forward. Mark stumbled back at his intense expression, eyes widening with a hint of fear. He'd always been able to intimidate the other man with his attitude and control. That control was slipping a bit. "Just because you signed an agreement doesn't mean anything."

"Then what was the reason for it?" Anger sliced hot into his voice. "She broke that agreement when she threatened me. If everything is settled, why did that bitch call me?"

Bitch? "You're calling her a bitch? After the way you treated her?"

His eyes widened again, and then narrowed in disbelief. "Fuck, you slept with her, didn't you?" Hard laughter roared out of his tight mouth. "Hell, look how far the high and mighty Lucas Benjamin has fallen. Getting with someone I've already had, many times."

He leaned in toward him and smirked. "So how'd you like the sloppy seconds?"

"What?"

"You heard me, little brother?"

Before his mind could tell him to stop, he flung up his fist and slammed it into his jaw. Mark's head jerked backward, body hitting into the desk before slumping slowly to the floor.

Luke glared down at his befuddled brother. Fear raced across his reddened features. He enjoyed seeing it. "Get up, asshole."

A large hand snatched at his fist and jerked it down. "That'll be enough, son."

"He's gone insane, Dad."

Luke twisted toward his father, forcing calmness and control back into his body. His hand loosened, fingers spreading wide as his father studied both of them.

"He assaulted—"

"Be quiet, Mark."

Anger rose again. "I should've done it long ago."

"Let it go, Luke."

Their father twisted from him toward his prone brother. Mark stood and brushed off his backside, rearranging his shirt and tie. "I only spoke the truth, Dad."

"Truth, Mark?"

Luke pressed his arms tight to his body, fighting the last of his temper. He'd never struck his brother before, but it felt good. He'd had it coming for a long time.

"Yes, Dad, I didn't say anything that wasn't true."

His father sighed. "I'm not even sure you can tell

the truth from fiction any more, son."

"Fiction is what Emma has Luke believing, Dad," he said, snorting a disgusted growl. "He believed her side of the story, and not mine."

"That's enough, Mark."

"Truth is truth, Dad."

Luke fought a renewal of his anger, forcing a calm breath into his lungs. He turned from his brother's flushed face and caught movement by the half-open door. A flash of blonde hair and a pale face appeared around the door for a second. Rebecca. Dad had brought Rebecca with him. But how did Dad know he'd come to force Mark to do the right thing?

Judge Brown. Was the judge somehow involved? Did he tell his father about his meeting with Mark?

Rebecca peeked around the corner again, sadness wet in her eyes. Luke sent a remorseful look her way before turning back to his brother.

"So let's hear your rendition of the truth, Mark." Both his dad and Mark glanced up at him, one set of eyes full of suspicion and the other with knowledge. Dad was more than aware of what he was up to. "You think Emma told me a made-up story. I think she's telling the truth, and you were lying."

Mark snorted and stepped around his desk, settling into his seat and leaning back. "How long did it take for you to sleep with her?" He smirked then. "Probably a little longer than it took me."

Luke's hands clamped together again. "The same amount of time it took for me and Kathleen, and we were happily married for over ten years."

"Yes, but Emma isn't a Kathleen." He jerked up from the chair. "Your wife was a decent woman who didn't jump from one man's bed into another's. If you think Emma will treat you any different than she did me, you're even a bigger fool than I thought. Woman like that just use men for what they can get out of them, and then leave."

"She's not like that," Luke said, hoping he was right and Mark wrong. "The only reason she told you about—"

Mark burst out in loud, mocking laughter as he stood from the seat. "Is she really pregnant? Or is she lying about that? Just because she comes to me with that ridiculous story doesn't mean I believed it." He snorted again. "Yeah, she claims she told me because she thought the father of the baby should know, but she didn't want anything from me. Then her lawyer puts a new stipulation in the agreement about a six-figure trust fund for the kid."

A low moan echoed from behind the door, a second before Rebecca stepped into the room. Tears ran down her flushed cheeks, heat of disappointment and anger showing clear in her expression. She raced past him and his father, and slapped Mark hard across his face. Then, without a word, she pulled off the engagement ring and flung it in his direction.

"Rebecca?"

His father touched her face lightly when she past him on the way out of the room, tender love showing on his rough, wrinkled features. "You're doing the right thing, Rebecca."

She just nodded and stepped away from them both before stopping at the door. Without looking back, she said, "It's over Mark. This time it's over."

"You don't mean that, honey."

Rebecca did look toward him then. "Have I ever taken off my ring before?"

The cockiness was gone from his face now.

"No," she said, voice choking through her renewed tears. "That's because I was hoping you would grow up. Yet that never happened. And it never will." She turned to the door, lowering her head. "Don't call me or my family, Mark. I don't want to have anything to do with you."

"Rebecca?"

Luke's best and oldest friend walked out the door, wiser and sadder, yet suddenly free.

"It's your fault, Luke."

"How can this possibly be your brother's fault?" Gentleness warmed his father's voice. "He's done nothing but take care of you since you were children."

"Yeah, the perfect son." Angry bitterness spoke loud in his words. "I'm nothing to you. Never have been."

"Son," his father said, beckoning for Luke to leave. "Mark and I need to talk—alone."

Luke nodded and wandered out of the room.

Dad needed to talk with Mark, and Luke needed to talk with Emma.

Dan sat behind his desk when he entered his office a few minutes later. He ignored him and raced into his sanctuary, snatching his coat and stepping through the outer office again. "Have something to take care of, Dan. I'll be back in an hour or so."

"Anything I can help you with, Luke?"

"No."

He sped toward the main entranceway door. Rain fell heavy around him as he stepped to his vehicle, dimming the afternoon sun gloomy as late night. He slipped into his car and backed out of the parking lot, spinning slightly on the wet pavement. He righted the vehicle and turned onto the main road.

Rain changed into snowflakes, falling so hard and fast his wipers couldn't keep up with the assault. Yet he didn't care. All he needed to do was drive a few miles to the catering business, to Emma.

Now that everything was out in the open, she would be willing to see him again.

****

Emma must not have heard Meg right. "Are you talking about the Benjamin/Greenlee wedding?"

"Yes."

"Rebecca called it off," she said, still not comprehending the conversation. "Didn't she and her fiancé just get back together?"

"Yes," Meg said, in a slightly gossipy way. "I heard she even gave him back the ring this time."

"Didn't she do that the other times?"

"I don't know," Meg said. "All I know is the last time she called off the wedding, she wasn't crying. I'm thinking she finally saw Mark for real. I almost feel sorry for her."

Why would Rebecca react that way? Did he tell her about the baby? If so, why did she call off the wedding? If Meg said the wedding was off, then it was off. That wedding planner had a special gift at knowing if two people would last or not. Emma had never known her to be wrong.

"Did she tell you the details?"

"No." She lowered her voice to a soft whisper. "Rumor has it her fiancé has never been faithful. I got

98

the impression she knew about his other women, and that's why she called off the wedding so many times. She must have been hoping he would see the error of his ways, but I guess that never happened."

Her heart hurt for the woman. "She's better off without him then."

"I think so too," Meg said, no more whispering secrets. "I was really looking forward to planning her wedding. It would've been good for my business."

"Oh, well," Emma said. "Women need to think of themselves sometimes. Without love, what do you have?"

"Sex," Meg said, with a short laugh. "But I know what you mean."

A knock sounded on the closed office door. Since when did her mom or sister knock? "Look, I have to go now. Someone's here."

"Okay, I need to get off the phone too." Determination rattled in her tone. "I've got to find another big wedding to plan in August. I'll talk to you later."

"Goodbye."

A second rap sounded. "Mom, Steph, stop making so much noise and come on in."

A dark shadow spread across the floor when the door opened, too big to be either her mother or sister. She froze. "What are you doing here, Luke?"

"Your mother said I could come on back," he said, not moving from the doorway. "I have good news."

"You're supposed to talk to my uncle," she said, not letting his low voice enchant her. She'd made up her mind not to see him again. Even if Mark somehow did the right thing, it would still be too uncomfortable to be around him. No matter how much she wanted it to work out, it just wouldn't. Unless she had an abortion, which she would never do, this baby would always come between them. Always. "He just left here a few minutes ago."

"I talked to him," he said, softly, still not moving from the doorway. "I told him what I'm about to tell you."

"I have nothing to say to you." She turned toward her computer screen. "You need to go away."

"No."

"No?" She jerked her chair back. "Maybe people who work for you have to put up with that type of thing, but I don't. I won't." She slammed her hand on her mouse. The icon on the screen disappeared and she sighed, moving the mouse in tiny circles until it reappeared near the bottom. "Just go, Luke."

"Not until I have my say." He unzipped his coat and shook off the light, wet snow before hanging it on a hook by the door. He sank into a visitor seat and placed one ankle over the other leg. "I'm going to have my say, Emma."

"Well, why not just sit down?"

"Thanks," he said, with that familiar, warm grin. "But I'm already sitting."

"Asshole," she whispered.

Luke laughed. "Such language."

Giving up the impossible task of getting him to leave, she crossed her arms. "Seeing that you're making yourself at home, you might as well tell me what you told my uncle. I'll decide if it's important or not."

"It's important, babe."

"Don't call me babe," she said, forcing away the

heat the simple word caused. She needed to get this man out of here before she did something really stupid. Like allowing him to talk her into believing everything would turn out fine. That only happened in fairytales. "So why did my uncle allow you to see me?"

His story came quick and concise, to the point. She fought back a smile when he said he punched his brother in the face. Then she had to force back tears a few short sentences later when he told about Rebecca throwing her ring at him. She barely knew the woman yet she felt for her.

"I came directly here," he finished. "By now I'm sure my mother and sisters know of your baby, and the gossips are fast spreading the news to the other family members. Soon everyone will know."

To Emma, that was the biggest problem. "I'm glad for Rebecca."

"Yes, so am I." He dropped his foot to the floor and leaned toward her. "I'm also glad for us, for you and me."

She shook her head, forcing back the flood of tears. "It doesn't change anything, Luke."

His brown eyes widened. "Yes, it does, babe. It may be uncomfortable at first while everyone is getting used to the idea of you carrying Mark's baby. But it'll be okay."

"Will you get used to it, though?" She slipped off the chair and moved around the desk, settling into the seat beside him. "You may think so now. But you'll always know that baby is your brother's. You'll be responsible for her or him if we end up staying together. You'll end up regretting it." She touched his hard arm. "I don't want that."

"It wouldn't matter to me," he said, softly. "You are that baby's mother and I…care about you."

Her heart cried at his confession, yet she silenced it. "No, you can't feel that way. We haven't known each other long enough."

"Yet, I do care," he said, a wash of desire and pain, of sweet love and disbelief raced across his eyes. "I love you, Emma. Crazy as it may seem, I do."

No, no, no. He couldn't love her. He only thought he did because… Because of what? Didn't he say he fell in love with his wife quickly too? Confusion darkened her mind, making it hard to think. She needed him to leave. She needed to get away from everything and everyone that reminded her of the last few months of mistakes. "I can't handle this now, Luke."

"I know you care for me, Emma."

His hand stroked her cold cheek, sending a rush of heat through the skin.

"That'll be enough for now."

"No." When she pulled her head back, he traveled his hand around her head, cupped it gently and leaned in close. Only a whisper of a breath touched her lips.

"My mom still wants to meet you, at Thanksgiving. We'll be at the Benjamin Wine booth at the festival. I'll leave you be until then so you can think."

She sighed. "I won't be changing my mind."

A flash of concern roared into his face before it emptied of all emotions. "Today is Monday." He traced his finger down her face and then stood and wandered to the door. "If you want to talk, I'll be helping my mother at her booth. I won't come to you." He grabbed his coat, opened the door, and stepped out. "If you want to give us a chance, tell me then. If you don't, I'll know it's over."

She couldn't say a word as his ultimatum sang in the air.

"Goodbye for now, Emma."

If she'd learned anything about this man in the short time she knew him, it was that he would be true to his word. If she wanted to move on with their relationship, she had to make the next move.

"Honey." Her mother touched her arm. "Are you okay?"

Emma nodded.

"Honey?"

She should be angry at his underhandedness, yet she wasn't. Hadn't she acted the same way with Mark? She threatened to tell Rebecca about the baby if he didn't, and yet now that the Benjamins knew, she still denied her feelings for Luke. She glanced at her mother. "Will you and Steph be okay here alone?"

"We'll be fine."

Emma shut down the computer and grabbed her purse from the desk drawer. "I need to leave."

"George told me what happened," she said, apprehension tightening her mouth. "Why did you chase Luke away?"

"That's why I need to leave early," she said, taking the coat from the hook. "I'm just not sure…"

Her mother sighed and pulled her into a tight hug. "Be careful driving home. The storm looks worse than everyone expected. Rain has turned into snow, and visibility isn't good."

"I'll be careful, Mom."

"Maybe you should spend the night at my house." She followed her into the store front. "Yes, you need to stay with me tonight. I'll get the house key. The exit from the highway to your street is too dangerous in this type of weather."

Her mother didn't wait for a response. She moved into the kitchen and disappeared in the back room. Emma tightened her garment and slipped out of the door, racing in the chilly air to her car. The vehicle roared to life a second later. She backed out of the parking space and turned onto the main road, ignoring her mother's frantic calls.

She loved her mother, yet tonight she needed to be alone.

Emma could barely see the road, even with the wipers racing across the windshield. She focused on the wavering lights of the vehicle in front of her until her turn came into view. Then she slowed and drove toward the cross road.

Her car careened forward so suddenly she jerked into the seatbelt and then slammed back into the seat. Another car hit the side, pushing her into a snowy depression, flipping the vehicle sideways. Emma screamed. The car jolted to a stop in a ditch. She hung upside down and at an angle, belt tight. Sharp pain raced through her.

She couldn't breathe.

"Don't move," a far-away voice spoke. "I've called 9-1-1. You need to stay still."

"Can't breathe," she hissed. "Can't…"

"Don't move," the vague voice said again.

Agony traveled through her, settling in her lungs. She fought to stay conscious.

"Stay still," the voice spoke again. Low and far away, Emma could barely understand. "What's your name?"

"Name?"

"Yes, tell me your name."

Her head hurt, along with her arm and rib area. And it was getting harder and harder to breathe.

"Tell me your name."

"Emma."

"Emma. You need to stay still, Emma. Help is coming."

The baby. Something's wrong with the baby. She needed to get the belt off now. She pressed the release button. It let go, slamming her hard onto the roof.

"Emma, no."

Blessed blackness followed the vague panicked words.

Chapter Ten

Emma slowly opened her eyes. Bright lights and sharp antiseptic smells filled her senses. Neutral colors came to view, then a few diagnosis machines. A plastic tube ran into her arm—an IV—while a second ran from another machine to her chest area. A black brace wrapped her arm, laying it flat on the bed beside her. Beeps and whirls echoed; beyond was the sound of voices and footsteps. Movement came from the side of the bed.

"About time you woke up, honey." Relief sounded in the beautiful voice, in the gentle touch of her hand "You scared us."

"I'm…sorry, Mom."

Deep wrinkles lined her mouth with her sad smile. "You did nothing wrong, honey."

"My…baby?"

A frown replaced the smile. "I'm sorry, honey. You lost the baby."

Tears washed over her face, in a flood filled with anger and hurt. Dull pain sliced through the slight movement "I…killed the baby."

"No," her mother said, in the no-nonsense voice she used when she disagreed with her. "It was an accident, honey."

"No, Mom." Emma wanted to believe her, yet she couldn't. Pain reverberated unhindered through her body, both physical and emotional. The baby was gone, the emptiness inside told her this truth more than her mother's words. Tears threatened. "I wanted…"

"Honey, you were in an accident." Her mother placed her hand against her cheek. "You didn't plan on getting into an accident, did you?"

A sob escaped her tight hold. "I…left you."

"Emma?"

She choked out words around her dry tongue. "If I'd…waited…for you, this wouldn't…"

"Emma Rose, that's enough.

"I…wanted an abortion."

Her mother stood and stepped from the bed, dragging in a few loud breaths. Then she returned quickly to the bedside and cupped both of her cheeks, bringing her face within a whisper of hers. "You are not at fault."

"But I…"

"Stop it right now, Emma." Anger tightened her hands against her face. "I will not allow you to say things like that. You would never be a part of murdering a baby, through an abortion or an intentional car accident."

Emma let that flow into her, yet. "But it does solve my biggest problem…"

"Luke?"

Emma nodded. "He confuses me, Mom."

"Oh?"

"Yes." When her mother didn't say or do anything, she sighed and said, "He's…caring. No man cared that much, not even Frank. Luke is…open with his feelings." She glanced up at her mother. "Like Dad."

Her mother studied her for a while before tapping

her cheek and settling in the chair near the bed. "Do you love him?"

"That's what so confusing," she said, finding the bed control and raising her head a little. Sharp, quick pains stabbed around her ribs. Her vision went fuzzy and dizziness washed over her. She took in a set of slow, easy breaths into her sore lungs. "Everything hurts."

Her mother frowned. "The doctor said you were lucky. You have a few broken ribs and your arm, of course. Your punctured right lung and the miscarriage…were the worst."

"This baby caused so many problems for me, yet it still…hurts." Emma placed her left hand on her flat stomach. "I feel…empty. Hollow." Tears sneaked from her eyes, dimming the image of her mother. "I…didn't want this to…happen."

The agony intensified, exploding like an egg in a microwave. Why did it hurt so much? She barely felt pregnant, barely had the chance to enjoy it. She'd never gotten past that beginning stage. She'd never gotten to the stage where she felt good.

"Did I ever tell you how your father and I met?"

Emma pushed her hurt away. "Only…a million times."

Happy sadness softened her voice. "We dated for three years before he asked me to marry him."

Emma knew that.

"But I knew he was the man for me way before that." She shook her head. "I fell in love with him two weeks after meeting him."

She didn't know that. "Really?"

"And he fell in love with me a week sooner."

Sweet laughter brightened the air. "We wanted to get married right away, but your grandparents thought we needed time to learn about each other."

"I didn't know that," Emma said, sensing the reason for the story now. "But that was a different time, Mom. Men were decent then, not assholes like Mark. Or Frank."

"So you're finally admitting your ex-husband wasn't perfect?"

"I never thought he was perfect, Mom." Emma pulled her hand from her stomach and rubbed the fingers of her other hand. "No one's perfect. I thought he was decent, however. Faithful."

Silence followed her comment. Not an uncomfortable perception at first, but it soon changed as the memory of her accident invaded her. Discomfort rushed in, both the physical aching and the emotional. It was the emotional distress that settled in her soul, darkening her world with thunderous clouds.

"I talked to your uncle," her mother whispered. "He told me he called Mr. Benjamin to tell him about Luke confronting his brother. Rebecca was on her way to Mark's office, so he allowed her to follow. The rest... Well, you know the rest."

"I figure Uncle George got involved somehow," she said.

"Are you upset at him?"

"No, I'm thinking it was the only way Rebecca would have found out." Emma said, patting the black cast lightly. "Luke told me she gave back the ring."

"Luke seems like a good guy, honey."

"Yes, he is." Emma would never deny that. She'd never met a man who showed his feelings so easily, and cared so much. And he really listened to her. "Maybe he's too good."

"Too good?" Her eyes narrowed and then widened. "You love him, don't you?"

"He's not Dad," Emma said. "And I'm not you. Love doesn't work that way any more. No one can fall in love after only seeing each other a few times."

She grinned. "Love happens in its own time, Emma. When two people are meant to be together, they know it. Like your father and I knew."

"But is that what's in the stars for Luke and me?"

Her mother didn't say anything for a few minutes before she smiled. "Luke told me about the ultimatum he gave you."

"He did?"

"I think you should take the time between now and before Thanksgiving dinner on Sunday," she said, leaning in close and touching her face lightly. "And decide if you want to take a chance on him or not."

"It's not enough time."

Her mother just patted her cheek and grinned.

****

Two days later, the doctor released Emma from the hospital.

"Be careful." Anxiety rode clear in her mother's voice. "My daughter's in a lot of pain."

"I will, Mrs. Cook."

Emma sighed. "I'll be fine, Mom."

The nursing assistant locked the wheelchair and held out her hand. "Ready to go?"

She nodded.

Dressed in a simple pull-on dress with non-slip slippers on her feet, the young woman helped her into the wheelchair and set her feet into the footrests. Numbness settled around her heart, keeping her from feeling emotional pain. Yet her body ached with the physical kind. Even with her arm secured in a sling tight to her body and a tight wrap around her ribs, pain stabbed her with every tiny movement. The narcotic she'd just received barely took the edge of it.

Oh, why couldn't her body be as numb as her heart?

The aide pushed her toward the door, sending another blast of discomfort through her. The older nurse followed. "Your daughter will be fine, Mrs. Cook."

"Yes." Her mother still looked worried. "It was a bad accident."

The nurse nodded. "But she's young and strong. In time, she'll heal."

Maybe her body would, but she wasn't sure about her heart. Her eyes watered and she placed her hand on her empty stomach.

"Some things heal quicker than others." Her mother waved the release form at the nurse. "I'll make sure Emma follows the doctor's instructions."

"That's good." The nurse glanced at the nursing assistant. "You may take her to the car now."

"And be careful," her mother said, a frown lining her mouth.

"Yes, Ma'am." The younger woman looked over at her uptight mother before grinning at Emma. "Are you ready to go?"

Emma nodded.

The nurse left them, and then the aide pushed her down the hall to the elevator, her mother moving close behind them. "My other daughter is waiting at the entrance for us."

The aide pushed her inside the elevator, holding the door for her mother. Emma closed her eyes, opening them again when they reached the ground floor. Soon she was outside. And instead of another stormy day, bright sunlight burned her eyes. All the freaky early winter snow had melted.

"Nice day." The aide pointed toward Steph's car. "Is that the right car?"

"Yes." Her mother stepped toward it and opened the front passenger side door. "I'll sit in the back with the boys."

The boys? Steph brought her children to pick her up?

Her nephews' presence tunneled under her numbness, threatening to push it aside. No, she required it. She needed to be strong until she was alone. Neither her mother nor her sister ever lost a child. They wouldn't understand her misery, especially when she herself wasn't sure why it hurt so much. She'd acted like she didn't want Mark's kid, even telling herself the same thing.

Yet it had all been a lie. Emma was a part of the baby too—a bigger part. This was the child she wanted more than anything. She just didn't realize it until the baby was gone.

"I'll help you," the aide said, forcing her mind off her interior struggles on to her exterior one. "Let me know when you're ready."

The door stood opened, with Steph leaning sideways and frowning at her. The boys were quiet in the back, with looks of childish concern. She looked at the seat. "I'm ready."

She stepped from the chair and settled into the car, sharp pain knifing into her ribs. The young girl smiled and disappeared.

The boys still didn't make a sound.

Her mother got into the back seat. "I'm ready to go, Steph."

Those were the last words any one said on the way to her home.

Twenty minutes later, Steph pulled into her driveway. She helped her out of the car toward the front door. "Will you be okay, Emma?"

Concern sounded in her voice, sadness darkened her eyes. "I'll…be fine."

"Mom or I could stay with you, if you want," she added. "Maybe you shouldn't be alone right now."

No, Steph was wrong. Right now, being alone was the proper thing to do. Being alone so she could cry out her pain was what she needed now. "I'll call you later."

"Promise?"

She nodded, fighting the prickling sensation of tears. "Yes."

"Okay." Steph placed her hand on the doorknob, but didn't close it.

Emma sighed. "Mom and your boys are waiting for you."

Wetness shined in her eyes a second before she raced to her and hugged her carefully. "I'm so sorry, Emma."

Tears did flow then, as if someone opened the floodgates of a dam. She took in a quick, few breaths and wiped her face, not wanting her sister to see her response.

"Bye." Steph slammed the door behind her.

Emma let go of her control then, falling to the sofa as the pain and anger roared from her.

Finally.

****

Saturday night, Mark dropped Luke at home. Exhaustion weighed on him like a five-story building. The two of them and Dad had been on the go in Cincinnati for the last three days, finalizing the addition of the latest acquisition to Benjamin Industries. It was a nice achievement for the business, a small, well-received pizza place on the outer limits of the city.

Yet he was more tired because of his brother's constant complaining about Rebecca than the tense schedule. As if Mark didn't have anything to do with her decision to call off the wedding. Many times Luke had bitten his tongue to keep from giving his opinion on the issue. To keep the family peace, he'd managed to make it through the last few days.

All he wanted now was sleep.

He'd planned on resting for only a few minutes, yet he'd drifted off. A distant ringing broke through his fatigue, pulling him from his half-slumber. His cell phone buzzed louder. He exhaled an unbelieving breath as he reached for it. "Hello."

"I'm sorry for calling so late, Luke."

The female voice woke him completely. He grinned as he shrugged out of his coat. "No problem, Rebecca. I almost fell asleep with my coat on."

Instead of a weak laugh at his lame joke, a choking sob echoed in the line. Shit, Luke didn't have the patience for a crying female right now. A teasing image of a woman standing naked near a kitchen door came to mind. He forced the picture away and focused on his phone call. Rebecca was right here, sobbing because of his asshole brother, no doubt. Emma was…not…and she may never be, near him again.

"It's your stupid fault, Benjamin." He grumbled into the phone. A shocked sob radiating into his ears and he quickly said, "What's wrong, Rebecca?"

"It's about…Emma," she said, between choked-back tears. "Her mother called your mother on Tuesday afternoon."

"Why?" He stood up straighter as the first part of her comment broke through his fatigue. "Did something happen to Emma?"

Her sobbing lasted for a few more seconds. "I told Mark about it and he was happy. Happy."

Luke was too tired for this game. "Told Mark what, Rebecca?"

"About Emma," she said, fighting for control again. "She was in a car accident Monday night."

He jerked up straight. "Is she all right?"

"She's fine, Luke." Concern lowered the tone of her voice. "But she lost the baby."

Emma lost her baby? Oh, please no. "How did you find this out? Are you sure?"

"Like I said, her mother called yours. Mom and I were visiting at the time." Now only professionalism rode in her tone. "And your mom called your dad late Tuesday night. Your dad didn't tell you?"

Now he understood why Mark seemed like a different person on the drive home. "No."

"I'm sorry," she said. "Mark knew so I just assumed you did."

Emma lost the baby?

"Mark wants me to take back his ring," Rebecca

said, hesitation in her voice. "I'm not sure what to do."

"You really love him, don't you?"

"I'm not sure any more."

Luke didn't know what to tell her. How could he help her when he couldn't even help himself? "I'm not in any position to give advice on love and marriage."

She stayed silent.

"I messed everything up with Emma," he admitted. "I gave her a choice the last time I saw her. I gave her a time limit to make up her mind about us. On Monday."

She didn't comment.

"Rebecca?"

"I just realized something, Luke," she said, sadness echoing in the phone line. "You are a much better man than Mark."

"No, I'm not. A good man wouldn't have upset his wife enough to speed in bad weather, or his lady."

"Neither Kathleen's nor Emma's accidents were your fault, Luke." Anger now. "If the situation were reversed, you would never tell Emma to take back your ring. You would never expect her to still marry you."

Guilt filled him. Rebecca had called him for comfort and he'd focused on his own selfish needs. He wandered into the bathroom and snatched a paper cup from the stack on the counter, sticking it under the spigot. The cool liquid soothed his throat.

"Emma wasn't the first woman he'd cheated on me with," she said, softly. "She's the first one that got pregnant, though."

"He'll never change, Rebecca."

"I know. But I hoped he would."

Peace filtered into him. "This one time I'm going to tell you what to do. Don't take back his ring. Let him go. Find a decent man."

"You're right," she said, through her sobs. "Maybe someday I'll find a man like you."

Luke grinned at the hint of strength in her. She would be all right. "You will."

"Right," she said with a forced laugh. "So will you be at the wine booth tomorrow?"

"Like always," he whispered. "Sunday too."

And he hoped Emma would approach him.

"I'll see you there then," she said, before whispering goodbye and ending the call.

"No, wait, I need—" Dead air sounded in his ear. "I need to find out if Emma is out of the hospital."

If the last few days had shown him anything, it was that he loved her. And he would fight to keep her.

Simple as that.

Chapter Eleven

"Get out of here, you two," Aunt Cora said. "We older folks can set up things fine without you. But be back before noon."

Steph nodded. "Let's go Emma while the going's good."

Emma would rather stay behind with her aunts and mother, but she allowed her sister to pull her out into the crowded floor. Rain fell with a thundering roar, reminding her of the accident. She shivered at the vague memories that still haunted her. Would she ever forget them? Her baby was gone, so probably not.

"Thank God the committee decided to hold the festival inside this year," Steph said, stopping in the middle of the community center's large room. "This looks even bigger than last year."

Emma nodded. Orange and black were the predominant colors with a sprinkling of yellow, red, and green. Five rows of long tables with yellow or green tablecloths sat in the center of the spacious building, with Thanksgiving themed decorations set every five or six feet. Along the front wall and the sides were colorful displays on tables with a mix of holiday themes, big signs hanging from the front or along the wall behind the tables with the names of the sponsors.

"Let's start at the left and work our way around." Steph took her arm and led her to the first display. "I plan on getting something from most of the sellers."

Emma forced a grin. "I believe you."

"This one looks promising," she said, stopping at the first seller. "Last year I got some pies from this church. Good."

"Nice display."

A big, fake turkey sat in the center of the table with loads of traditional meal fixings around it. Fluffy potatoes with gravy and green beans, red cranberries, and corn looked so real Emma could almost taste them. On either side were warm pies and plates of cookies, real deserts covered in plastic wrap and ready to be sold. The sign leaning against the table read in big bold letters: All Money will be Donated to the Church's Christmas Fund. Please be Generous.

"I'm going to buy more than one of these pies this year." Steph picked up two apples and a pumpkin. She smiled at the older woman behind the table. "These are so good."

"Thank you," the woman said. "Everything we sell is wonderful."

"Yes, I bet." Steph paid and accepted the plastic bag. "Next."

Emma followed her sister to the next table, where she brought two-dozen chocolate chip cookies and added them to the bag. They moved to the next table. Steph breathed in deep. "I'm in heaven."

"You look it," Emma said. "You won't have to bake anything for a few months at the rate you're going." A hint of peace filled her. "And you love baking."

"Okay, you caught me," she said, stepping to an older man dressed as a pilgrim in all black. She paid for a plate of brownies and backed away from the table. "Mason's family members and some friends go to the churches I buy from, so I thought I'd help them with their charity."

Emma grinned. The real joy issuing from her sister eased her ache a bit more. "Giving to charity isn't a bad thing, Steph."

"I never said it was." She swung the plastic bag at her. "I'm going to help some other charities now."

Her sister was in her element. Just about every other table had a sign that mentioned collecting money for different charities. Homemade dog and cat toys sat on a table for the Animal Rescue of Bridgeview; a little further, another church held a bake sale for Christmas; beyond that was a booth collecting donations of gently used clothing and toys for children. Steph promised the woman she would gather some of her boys' things and drop them at their office. They reached the end of the side and turned toward the first booth against the front wall.

"Now things for the adults," Steph said, arching her eyebrows. She stopped and looked around. "Ah, here we are."

Emma had been focusing on a Native American thanksgiving display on a table a few feet away when her sister suddenly stopped. Emma crashed into her back. "Hey, be careful."

"Oops, sorry." Steph didn't sound sorry at all. "I've always wanted to try this wine," she added, slipping to her side. "Said its award-winning stuff."

"You don't drink—" Emma's mouth dried. "Luke?" A small woman stood beside him.

"Hi, Emma."

Steph accepted a plastic glass from the smiling older woman and took a small sip, making a face. "Dry."

"We have sweeter varieties." The woman stepped away from Luke toward her sister. "Would you like to sample one of those, Stephanie?"

Emma glared at her sister. "Mrs. Benjamin knows your name?"

"Of course, dear." She pressed into Luke's side, a look of cunning knowledge in her eyes. "Luke, I'll take care of her sister. You help your lady."

His lady? Emma's heart raced. More than anything *his lady* was what she wanted to be, but it wasn't right to be delighted by her knowledge. She barely knew the man.

"Go on, Luke," his mother said. "You must not leave a customer unattended."

"Mom?"

"Better yet." She pushed his arm. "You need to take a break. You've been no help to me at all today."

He looked as startled as Emma felt at his mother's brashness. Luke gathered his wits before she realized what was happening, and nodded. "I'll be back soon, Mom."

"No need." Her smile extended to Emma before she smirked at Steph. "Your sisters and father will be here soon."

"I just bet they will," he said, obvious affection mixed with the hint of skepticism in his words. Then only his love shined in his eyes. "Thank you, Mom."

"You're welcome."

Emma had a hard time taking her eyes off him as he walked around the booth. He looked so good in his tight faded jeans and simple T-shirt. Maybe a bit tired and sad, yet he still looked good.

Sad? Does he know about my accident? About me losing the baby?

"I could use some coffee." He lifted his hand toward her and then dropped it. "I got home late last night, and had to get up early this morning to help bring in the wine. Yesterday they sold out completely."

He waved his hand, indicating she should precede him toward the coffee booth at the end of the back row of steaming buffets. Her mother looked pleased when they walked past the buffet table. Was her mother in on Steph and Luke's Mom's deception? Probably.

"Every year I have to replenish the booth. Mom always misjudges how much people love her wine."

"Mom and the aunts never do that." Emma kept her focus on the people in front of her. She stopped behind an older lady and waited her turn. "I could use a cup of coffee. I didn't…sleep well, either."

He touched her then, a light brushing of his hand down her arm. Shivers spread in the places his fingers caressed, warming her for a brief instant. The woman got her coffee and moved from the table. Emma stepped to the front of the line. Luke paid and handed her a cup before taking her elbow lightly and striding toward the end of one of the long tables. He pulled out a chair for her.

"Thank you."

He nodded and stepped around the table, settling in the seat across from her. He sipped his coffee, obviously waiting for her to speak. The sharp scent of the dark liquid drifted toward her. The darkness under his eyes and lines around his mouth showed he spoke the truth about not sleeping. She set down her cup and reached toward him, freezing for a second before touching the darker skin under his eyes.

"Look that bad?"

She traced her fingers down to his chin, and then dropped her hand. "I was supposed to talk to you first."

"You did, babe."

"Saying your name isn't talking to you." She sipped her coffee. "Did you know your mother knew my sister?"

Luke shrugged, but didn't answer. He just considered her around the coffee cup, sadness in his eyes and a slight frown on his face. He sipped the liquid, knuckles tightening around the cup. His gaze traced along her sling to her ribs until they focused on her middle. Then he lifted his eyes to her face. Tension roared off him like wave after ocean wave.

Say something, Luke.

Still, he stayed quiet.

"You know about…"

"Yes."

She sensed his tight control, his patient power. "It…hurts."

"Yes." He touched her tense hand and then placed his fingers back around the cup. "You broke your arm?"

"And a few ribs," she said, fighting to keep the tears away. "My right lung was also punctured. The doctor said I got to the hospital in time to repair that, but…"

"But?"

Tears did fall then. "They couldn't save my baby."

"I'm sorry, babe."

"Babe?" His image wavered in her vision as the

tears overflowed, falling unhindered down her cheek to hang for a brief second on her chin. He brushed them away, setting his hand light on the sling. She focused on his caring touch. "My heart aches. I didn't think it would...hurt so much."

"So does mine," he said, eyes shining with unshed tears in response to her pain. "I know he was my brother's child, yet it was..."

"What?" She needed to hear it. She needed to hear him say it. "It was what?"

"Also yours." He stepped around the table and crouched beside her, placing his hand lightly on her middle. "That's why I hurt."

She loved this man. It didn't matter if they met less than a month ago. Her parents had fallen in love almost at first sight too, and they had a good life together for over thirty years. It didn't matter if she'd made the mistake of sleeping with his brother when she was drunk and depressed. Mark didn't matter.

Luke placed his hand under her chin and raised her head. "You probably don't know this, but my mom went to the hospital to see you."

"She did?"

"She waited until your mom and sister left," he said, moving his spread hand to the back of her head. "She was hoping to get away before they returned, but didn't make it in time."

"They never told me," she said. "Our moms talked?"

"Yes." A mysterious look brightened his sad eyes. "I just found that out a few minutes ago."

"So that's how they knew each other."

His grin widened. "Seems like it."

She should be pissed at her sister. How dare she connive to get the two of them together? How dare Mom and Luke's mother go along with it? Everything was resolved like she wanted when she called Mark that morning, yet that didn't change anything. His brother still got her pregnant. The Benjamins would always know that.

Luke deserved better.

"Mom asked your mother to Thanksgiving dinner," he said, an enigmatic, slightly alarming look in his eyes. "And she accepted the invitation for both of you."

"She shouldn't have, Luke."

"Why?"

"Why? Why do you think?" Keeping anger inside at a situation that was mostly resolved wasn't an easy thing. So why try? Why not let go and see where things landed? Just the question eased her mind. "We barely know each other."

"So?"

One of his fingers slid to her mouth, caressing her bottom lip until tingles raced through her. Her body remembered this man's touch. When his lips replaced his finger in a gentle kiss, she let go of the last of her apprehension. He growled her name and deepened the kiss, lifting her to encircle her arms loosely around him.

"Well, will you look at them?"

Emma clutched his T-shirt at the sound of her sister's laughing voice. Luke let go of her mouth and twisted her around to face her smirking sister and tearing-up mother. Both his hands spread wide on her stomach.

"You're not allowed to do that, honey." Her mother choked out the words. "I read the instructions from the doctor. No sex for six weeks."

"That's fine with me."

"Good." Another pleased voice spoke from behind them. Mrs. Benjamin patted her son's back as she moved past them and stopped between her mother and sister. "That will give us all time to get to know each other better." She smiled gently at her. "Time enough to settle any mistakes from the past so we can move into the future. Past is the past."

No tears came at Luke's mom's tentative acceptance, yet Emma's aching heart yielded a bit. In time, she hoped to have her approval. She hoped all the Benjamin clan would forgive her past actions and receive her completely.

"Let's get out of here before she starts crying again." Steph linked arms with both their mothers and led them toward the right wall. "I need to finish giving to charity before Mason shows up and stops me."

Their laughter roared until they wandered into the colorful displays.

"You're not going to cry again?" he asked.

"No," she said, twisting easily to face him. "Not now, but I might later."

"I'm glad, babe." His whispered words brushed over her mouth. "Because I love taking care of you."

And she loved him taking care of her. She grinned up at him and wrapped her good arm around his neck. "Even if we can't have sex?"

"No, we make love." He groaned out a sound of frustration. "And, yes, even if we can't do that."

Would things work out between them? She didn't know.

Only time would tell.

A word about the author...

Theresa Stillwagon has been writing most of her life. Since one of her teachers praised a poem she wrote for a class assignment in the eighth grade, she's been putting words together in the hopes of seeing them in print, not caring if anyone other than herself ever read them.

Her dream came to reality in 2008 when she signed her first writing contract. She has since followed that with a dozen more, including two series and a few standalone romances.

Bored with life in Ohio, Theresa and her husband Mike bought an RV and started traveling around the country with their cats, living and working in campgrounds. She enjoyed the lifestyle yet decided to give it up a half a dozen years later. Theresa and her husband, along with their cat, settled down in Georgia, near Savannah. The heat in the state was too much for her, so she moved back to her home state three years ago.

Her husband bothers her to no end and her cat, Frankie, bites her for no apparent reason, yet she's happy.

www.theresastillwagon.com